Dear Readers,

One of the nicest things about the Bouquet line is the burgeoning of a multitude of brand-new blossoms we're cultivating in our newly seeded garden of love. Four of them have burst into bloom this month, just in time for a fabulous fall flowering.

Take a woman hiding, under an assumed name, in a small Maine town, and a man hiding from life itself; add the rescue of a couple of cute kids, and you have Wendy Morgan's debut romance, **Loving Max.**

Grab a bikini and head for the tropics. Roast beef meets tofu when flower child Tasha and button-down salesman Andrew Powell III meet at a singles resort in Maddie James's rollicking romance, **Crazy For You.** Then, in Michaila Callan's **Love Me Tender,** travel to small-town Texas, where Eden Karr employs a handsome carpenter to redesign her boutique . . . and gets a new design for living and loving as well! Finally, fly to faraway, fantastical Caldonia, where New York magazine editor Nicole is hired to find a queen for handsome Prince Rand—before the end of the year—in **The Prince's Bride** by Tracy Cozzens. Will his coach turn into a pumpkin before her mission is accomplished . . . or will love find a way?

Speaking of pumpkins, we'll be back next month with four splendid new Bouquet romances—in brilliant fall colors. Look for us!

The Editors

COOKIES AND KISSES

"So now that I've told you my adventures as a would-be Martha Stewart . . . do you bake?" he asked, fighting the most irrational impulse to brush away a sugary cookie crumb that was caught on her lip.

"Me? Sometimes. When I need a chocolate fix and we're out of Oreos."

Finally, she had answered one of his questions without making him feel as though he'd invaded her life. "Oh, yeah?" He took a sip of coffee, needing to take his eyes off that damn crumb. "What's your specialty?"

"Cream cheese brownies."

"With powdered sugar or chocolate frosting on top?"

"Are you kidding? Frosting. And not from a can."

There was something flirtatious about her now, as though she'd forgotten her problems, whatever they were. As though she'd let down her guard and let the real Olivia emerge—the Olivia he'd sensed was there all along.

She wasn't exactly lighthearted or animated as they discussed the merits of homemade frosting versus canned, but she had finally relaxed a bit. That was why, when there was a lull in the conversation, he found himself saying, "You have a crumb on your lip."

It was an inane statement, really. The kind of thing he would do with one of the kids.

Just . . .

Reach out and brush the crumb away.

That was all he meant to do.

But when his thumb made contact with her soft, moist lower lip, he knew he had to taste it. He had to kiss her. He had to . . . or he would go out of his mind.

He moved his hand from her lips to the back of her neck, tangling his fingers in her hair, and he pulled her face toward him. He leaned in and his mouth closed over hers. Her lips were cookie-sweet and as silky soft as her hair, and they parted beneath his so easily that he was caught off guard.

It was as though she, too, had been anticipating this, as though she wanted it as much as he did. . . .

LOVING MAX

WENDY MORGAN

ZEBRA BOOKS
Kensington Publishing Corp.

http://www.zebrabooks.com

ZEBRA BOOKS are published by

Kensington Publishing Corp.
850 Third Avenue
New York, NY 10022

Zebra and the Z logo Reg. U.S. Pat. & TM Off.

First Printing: October, 1999
10 9 8 7 6 5 4 3 2 1

Printed in the United States of America

ONE

Olivia Halloran rounded a bend, following the jogging path as it emerged from the sheltering woods onto the open cliff high above the rocky beach. Instantly, an icy wind whipped off the sea and sliced through her.

It's a warning, she thought, bending her head and pulling the sleeves of her sweatshirt jacket lower on her thin wrists as she ran along.

Though it was merely mid-October, barely a month into autumn, the wind was a chilling reminder that winter was indisputably on its way.

And after several years of living on the northern Maine coast, Olivia was fully aware that the change of seasons wasn't to be taken lightly here. In the months ahead, the picturesque village of Newberry Cove would fall victim to short, dark days and bitter cold and snow. Tons of snow.

Growing up in balmy Los Angeles, she used to wistfully fantasize about what it would be like to skim down white-blanketed hills aboard a toboggan and skate on a frozen pond and catch lacy snowflakes on her tongue.

She'd pictured herself bundled cozily into fuzzy red mittens with a matching beret like the ones her best friend Debbi Olsson had bought during a Thanksgiving visit to her grandparents in Minnesota.

She'd imagined sugar-frosted Christmas mornings

when the world would look as Bedford Falls had in her favorite movie, *It's A Wonderful Life*, adrift and glistening with snow.

But Olivia was, by birthright, a sun-bleached beach blonde, the only child of thin-blooded native southern Californians who'd had no desire to venture anywhere, ever, where they'd be required to conceal their hard-earned physical perfection beneath insulating layers of wool and down.

In fact, her parents had insisted on spending Christmas in Waikiki every year. There, the one thing that glistened was the dark tanning oil on sculpted bronzed bodies; the only drifts consisted of fine Hawaiian sand.

There was no sand on this stretch of ocean beach.

Olivia contemplated this as she moved along the narrow path along the choppy gray water. At least, not abundant sand like you saw on the Pacific coast or in Daytona, Florida, which Olivia had once visited as a child.

Here, there were rocks—enormous boulders, pebbles, and shards of slate that hurt Olivia's bare feet and never seemed to warm beneath the summer sun.

She didn't necessarily *miss* the sand, though. She loved this northern beach just as it was; sometimes even felt as though it belonged to her alone. She'd never felt that way back home about Malibu or Redondo.

Just last week, when the weather had warmed to a glorious golden Indian summer, Olivia had sat, utterly, peacefully *alone*, on the bench-shaped gray slab at the edge of the water right down there, staring vacantly for over an hour at the lobster boats that bobbed out on the charcoal-blue water. That seaside perch was a perfect spot for daydreaming, for remembering what life had been like a few short years ago, when she hadn't been Olivia Halloran . . .

When her hair hadn't been dyed this unnatural pale

shade and her body had been all gentle curves instead of sharp angles; when her skin had been sun-kissed instead of this pasty color that revealed too clearly the circles that always, always rimmed her eyes these days—eyes that had once been what her father admiringly called "true blue." Now their hue was carefully, constantly hidden behind dirt-colored contact lenses.

Olivia didn't like to remember the past, *her* past, and yet it haunted every waking moment of her life; even haunted her when she finally managed to fall into an exhausted, fitful sleep in her solitary bed. It crept in after dark like an unwelcome intruder and filled her nightmares with memories of what and who she had once been.

Oh, the nightmares weren't as regular as they once had been. There were times when she actually closed her eyes in the wee hours and went to sleep and slept soundly for a few solid hours until morning.

But there were other times, more frequent times, when images rushed at her as she slept, when she saw faces of people who were long dead or faces of those who wished *she* were dead. She saw raised fists and a familiar, taunting voice, and she saw herself, blond and young and terrified . . .

There were times when faraway voices called her name, called "Katie . . . Katie?" Sometimes it was her parents or her friends who beckoned her, and sometimes it was *he,* and sometimes it was she herself, her own voice calling for Katie . . .

Long lost Katie Kenrick, the carefree girl who would forever be buried with the past.

Only Olivia Halloran trudged onward, waking every morning to life in a place she'd never chosen for herself and her young son, T.J.

Yet it felt strangely right for them now, foreign as it

was to the existence they had once known. She had learned to lose herself in the windy gray days and the slow-moving rural pace and the routine predictability that made it impossible to imagine any disruption. You couldn't imagine urban violence finding its way to this godforsaken spot with its miles of rocky coast and deep-green forests.

This world was safe . . . at least, it *seemed* safe. As safe as Olivia and T.J. Halloran were ever going to be.

Besides, she thought as the brisk wind picked up, she had her snow now. Never again would she long to know what a winter wonderland was like.

She had caught countless snowflakes on her tongue, and she had woken on many, many mornings to a fairyland Frank Capra scene outside her window. She had her white Christmases and her red fuzzy mittens and even her ice skates, a used pair she'd picked up for two dollars at a tag sale in September.

She had bought T.J. new ones last Christmas, and he had swiftly become an expert on the ice, gliding and careening along in a carefree way that had seemed to beckon her as she stood watching him, day after day, from the edge of the makeshift local rink. Now she would have her chance, in just a few more weeks. She would put on her skates and they would go to the rink together, and maybe she, too, would have a sense of being reckless and free—if only for a few fleeting moments.

The air smells like snow, she realized, taking a deep breath and slowing her pace slightly as the path became rough with jutting tree roots and jagged boulders.

She had been over this ground so many times that she expertly maneuvered over the bumps now, concentrating not on the path but on the notion that winter might put in an early appearance tonight. Her beat-up Chevy needed snow tires and she hadn't yet installed the storm windows in her drafty old house. She'd better get home and get busy or . . .

Or maybe it was just my imagination, she decided. *It's so early for snow . . .*

And yet, October storms were hardly unheard of in this region.

Olivia had no idea what the weather forecast had been for today.

She rarely watched the news these days, hardly ever picked up a paper.

There had been a time, long ago, when she had followed politics and sports and celebrities with interest, when the world around her had seemed full of fascinating people and events.

Now she wanted only to escape the reality that infiltrated the news and reminded her of things she'd rather forget. She didn't want to know about gang shootings or ten-year-olds on drugs or abandoned babies. She shielded herself from reports about plane crashes and deadly epidemics and the polluted planet. She could care less about cheating actors or corrupt politicians or abusive athletes.

It was best, she had realized, to worry only about yourself and your child, about what you had to do to survive from day to day. Best to mind your own business and not worry about things that didn't directly affect you.

"Help!"

Olivia blinked.

The faraway sound had been carried to her ears on the wind, so faint that she decided she'd been hearing things and jogged on.

"Help!"

Olivia frowned slightly and stopped on the path, poised, her head tilted as she listened.

Had that been a cry for help?

She heard it again, coming from below, across the

water, along with a splashing sound. A rocky, tree-dotted point jutted just ahead, shielding her view of the beach.

Her heart began to pound.

Someone was in trouble.

A child.

She knew that, instinctively, from the high pitch of the voice.

It wasn't T.J. She was sure of that. She had left him back at Dr. Klimek's office, where he was assisting the elderly veterinarian in bottle-feeding two tiny, orphaned puppies whose mother had been hit by a car.

No, T.J. was safe.

But a child, somebody's child, was in trouble on the water.

She hesitated only a moment before breaking into motion—this time not jogging but running, running toward the break in the trees up ahead where a path led down to the beach and the helpless little one on the water.

As she hurled herself down the incline and emerged on the rocky shore, she caught sight of the child . . .

The children.

There were two of them; oh, Lord, *two* tiny children adrift on some sort of makeshift raft in the choppy sea.

They weren't that far out—maybe thirty feet—but Olivia knew there was a steep drop-off and that the water there was deep.

"We can't swim! Please, lady, can you help us?"

One of the children had caught sight of her and was shouting to her, waving his arms wildly, which caused the raft to pitch dangerously. She could see the other small figure lying facedown, clinging to the rough boards. Two bedraggled ribbons hung down her back, fastened at the bottom of long blond braids. The sound of terrified whimpering reached Olivia ears.

"Hang on!" Olivia screamed at the children, sprinting

out onto the weathered, rickety pier. "Just try to stay still!"

She heard barking and saw that a puppy was paddling excitedly beside the raft, his frantic yelps summoning her to the rescue.

"Please, lady . . . Hey, Lindsey, look out. You're—"

There was a scream and a splash and the child who had been clinging facedown to the raft slipped overboard.

"No!"

Olivia shouted in unison with the other child, the boy, who had still somehow managed to maintain his balance on the raft.

Without stopping to think, she reached the edge of the water and kept going, splashing into the frigid ocean just as the second child fell off the raft while stretching and reaching for the little girl.

Olivia gasped as a painfully icy wave swept over her head, sending a fierce, sudden ache through her body so that she could barely move, could barely think. She sputtered and her feet found their balance in the slippery rocks on the bottom, the water sloshing against her chin as she glanced around for the children amidst the dog's frenzied barking and splashing.

Olivia caught sight of a bobbing blond head—oh, God, just one—and set out toward it. Her clothes were like weights pulling her down, and the current tossed her body as she plunged onward, but she did what she had been trained to do so many years ago as a California lifeguard. She swam swiftly, her strong arms pulling her forward, slicing rhythmically through the surf, and she kep* her eyes fixed on the struggling victim who kept bobbing in and out of sight.

Finally she reached the child, grabbing hold of a blond pigtail just before it disappeared beneath the greenish-gray swell again. She pulled the child up so that her face

Wendy Morgan

was out of the water, and she quickly tucked the tiny body under her arm, then glanced about for the other child.

There he was, in the water but clinging to the edge of the raft a few feet away. His head had been hidden by the planks.

Olivia exhaled a shivery breath of relief and swiped at the salt water streaming over her face, into her eyes.

"My sister!" he screamed at Olivia. "Where's my sister?"

"I have her," she hollered back, and caught sight of a rope dangling in the water nearby. She realized it was attached to the raft and grabbed it.

"I'm going to pull you to the beach," she instructed the little boy, who only nodded, his eyes wide and terrified. The dog's head bobbed beside him, and the animal's barks rode above the howling wind and waves.

Olivia realized that the only way to pull the raft was with her teeth, and she quickly bit down on the soggy length of rope.

Then, holding the little girl close to her side with her left arm and paddling with her right, she started towing them toward the shore, the dog swimming right beside her.

It was an endless, exhausting chore.

Waves washed over Olivia's head and her limbs were numb with cold and exhaustion. She wanted to look back to make sure the little boy was still holding on to the raft, but she couldn't risk moving her head and losing her grasp on the rope. There was nothing to do but keep moving, keep pulling toward the shore.

Finally, when she was a few yards away, her feet struck the rocky bottom again. She stood and grabbed the rope as she turned, terrified that she'd see an empty raft behind her.

But the child was there, his towhead plainly visible over the jagged planks.

"Can you hang on a minute longer?" Olivia called to him, and was gratified when his head lifted up and down in a feeble nod.

She forced her feet to carry her and her cargo through the water until she reached the beach.

For the first time, she glanced down at the face of the child tucked into her arm. The little girl's eyes were closed, her lips blue, her face ghostly.

Panic darted through Olivia as she lay the child on the beach.

The boy kept screaming about his sister, and Olivia bent over the still figure of the unconscious child.

"Please lady, save her! You have to save her," the little boy begged, clinging to Olivia's arm as she reached out to tilt the child's head back to open an airway.

Save her . . .

You have to save her . . .

You have to save her . . .

Please . . .

She worked systematically, administering CPR, pumping the tiny chest and blowing air from her own shivering mouth through the girl's purplish lips. She was vaguely aware of the howling wind and the sobbing little boy and the barking dog in the background, but her entire being was consumed by the need to force life back into the small, limp body.

Finally, she heard a faint gasp, and then the little girl's fragile chest gave a great, heaving shudder. She began to choke, her tiny frame moving in violent, jerking spasms.

Olivia cradled her as she fought to clear her lungs of the salt water she had swallowed; held her close against her breast and rocked her, murmuring to the terrified child that she was going to be all right; everything was going to be all right.

Inwardly she was uttering a fervent prayer of thanks that she had done it, somehow; that there would be a happy ending.

"You saved her, lady!" the little boy announced through chattering teeth, bringing Olivia back to full awareness. "You're, like, a real live hero. Wow, it was just like on *Baywatch*.

Olivia glanced at him, saw that his face was identical to the girl's. Both had wide-set green eyes and upturned noses covered by a splattering of pale freckles and pointy little chins.

Twins. They were twins, about T.J.'s age. They couldn't be more than six years old.

What were they doing alone on the beach? Where were their parents? Didn't they know the world was too full of dangers to ever let precious children out of their sight?

Fury mingled with Olivia's relief, and she wiped at the salty liquid that streamed down her cheeks, not knowing whether it was only seawater or if it mingled with tears.

She was overwhelmed, unable to move or respond, her body trembling violently all over.

"Boy, is Daddy going to be mad," the little boy told his sister, who still looked too dazed to react. She huddled against Olivia, her little fist clutching the soggy fabric of Olivia's jacket. She was sniffling, whimpering faintly.

"Where is your father?" Olivia was finally able to speak and discovered that her voice didn't sound anything like her own. It was a thin warble, quavery as she felt.

The boy shrugged. "He's home sleeping. Me and Lindsey were sailing around the world."

Olivia frowned. "What about your mother?"

"Dead," he said matter-of-factly, then added, "But you kind of look like her picture. Doesn't she, Lindsey?"

The little girl nodded, regarding Olivia through solemn eyes.

"You're not an angel, are you?" the boy asked abruptly. "Like, you're not our mother, visiting from heaven, are you? Because Daddy said she's watching over us."

Olivia's heart lurched. "No," she managed. "I'm not your mother. But I'm sure your dad is right. I'm sure she is watching over you.

"Maybe. Lady watches over us, too." The boy patted the dog, who sat wagging her tail beside them. "She's the greatest dog in the world. She takes care of us."

"She does." The little girl spoke for the first time, her head bobbing in agreement again. "We just got her a few weeks ago for our birthday, but Lady already takes care of me and Sam. Daddy says she's going to be like one of the family. Daddy's gonna be *really* mad, Sam."

Again, Olivia wanted to ask about their father, but a sound from the path above stopped her.

It was a shout.

She looked up to see an elderly couple scurrying toward the path on the incline, weaving among the trees above.

"Who are they?" the boy, Sam, asked Olivia.

"I . . . I have no idea." Trepidation stabbed into her, and she swiftly but gently moved the little girl off her lap and stood.

"I have to go now," she told the children, moving away from them.

"But you can't," Sam protested as his sister cried out "no!" and tried to grab onto Olivia's jacket again.

"I have to," Olivia repeated urgently, her voice rising as panic seeped in.

The elderly couple were moving with surprising speed for their age. They had nearly reached the beach.

You have to get out of here. Go. Go!

"Goodbye," Olivia hurriedly told the protesting children, then turned and jogged away along the rocky shoreline, careful not to twist an ankle on the uneven terrain.

Her legs felt wobbly, as though they could give out at any moment. She forced them to keep moving, to carry her along, away from the shouts of the elderly couple and the children, away from the dog, who was barking again.

Wait! Wait! Stop!

But she couldn't wait.

She couldn't stop.

Olivia clenched her teeth to keep them from clattering violently. She spotted another path sloping back up toward the jogging path, so she hurried in that direction and she got back on the path and ran and ran and ran . . .

Her thoughts careened wildly, and she offered yet another ardent, desperate prayer . . .

Please, please don't let them follow me.

Please don't let them find me.

Please, let them leave me alone . . .

As she ran, she told herself that none of them knew her name—not the children and not the elderly couple. They had all been strangers, probably weekend tourists.

She was safe.

You're safe.

You're safe.

Don't be a fool. Relax. Everything is fine. Just get yourself back to Dr. Klimek's office to get T.J. and then get home.

All she had done was jump into the water and rescue a couple of kids.

There was no reason that incident had to threaten her safety in any way . . .

And yet.

And yet, it had disrupted the everyday pattern, the

treasured tranquility of life in her little corner of the world.

What if . . .

"No!" She hurled the word aloud into the chilly autumn dusk as she jogged up the winding road that led away from the water, back toward the distant stone cottage where Dr. Klimek had his practice.

"No!"

No, she was safe.

Nothing had changed.

No one knew who she and T.J. really were.

No one would ever know.

She had no reason to succumb to fear.

But that night—long after Olivia had tucked T.J. cozily into bed and had taken yet another hot bath and drunk her steaming tea and swaddled herself in thermal clothes and burrowed beneath her thick down comforter—her body was convulsed with shivers.

She knew the violent trembling had nothing to do with the chill of the water or the windblown October snow that blew around the drafty old house.

And when she finally drifted off to sleep, the nightmares were back, more vividly terrifying than ever.

She was a beautiful angel, Daddy . . . and she looked like Mommy. Do you think it was Mommy?

As his daughter's question swept through his head again, Max Rothwell grimaced, something he hadn't allowed himself to do in front of Lindsey.

He had sworn that he would never tell the children the truth about Julia. No matter what. Better to let them believe that she was a beautiful angel watching over them from heaven than to tell them the truth about the mother they couldn't remember.

Julia had been beautiful, all right.

But he knew she wasn't the one who had saved Sam and Lindsey today. Not just because he didn't believe in heaven or angels, but because if Julia really were a spirit and if she did come back to earth for any reason at all, it sure as hell wouldn't be to save her children.

No, it would be to haunt and torment him.

So far, that hadn't happened.

For a long time after her death, he had kept expecting to turn around and see her or hear her. But he no longer heard echoes of her voice mocking his every word and he no longer thought he glimpsed her perfect face—a face distorted, in his eyes, by that perpetual pout.

No, Julia was gone, thank God.

Max had no idea who had saved his two children out on the water today. Until now, he had been so shaken by what had happened that he hadn't even allowed himself to wonder about her.

He had been sleeping in his easy chair by the fireplace when a knock on the door had awakened him. Sitting bolt upright, he had realized that the fire he'd built on the hearth had gone out and the room was cast in shadows that meant it was late afternoon.

Late afternoon?

How could it be?

As he staggered to the door, rubbing the sleep from his eyes, he called for the twins. They had been sitting on the floor at his feet the last thing he knew, playing with the toy globe he'd bought them—spinning it and giggling and whispering to each other in their own private coded language.

He realized he must have fallen asleep and knew, even as he hurried to the door, listening for their answering voices, that the house was empty. He'd left the dead bolt in place when they returned from their walk in the woods earlier, and now it was standing open.

Panic had sliced through him when he spotted the police car, red domed light circling, parked in the long, rutted drive.

Once before, he had been awakened from a sound sleep by a police officer's knock at the door.

Then, it had been 3:00 A.M., and his old childhood friend Andy Polucci, now a Newberry Cove cop, had come to tell him that Julia had been killed in a car wreck fifty miles away.

Today, when he found Andy standing on the other side of the glass, Max saw a familiar grim expression beneath the visor of his blue police hat.

His heart had lurched into his throat and he knew, in the moment that followed, that if something had happened to his children, he couldn't go on. Not this time. There would be no picking up the pieces, no fresh start.

If he had lost Lindsey and Sam, he had lost his very reason for existing.

He had fumbled for the knob with a trembling hand, thrown open the door—

And there they were.

Standing on either side of Andy, wrapped in enormous woolen blankets, their hair matted and wet.

At first, all he cared about was that they were alive.

He hauled them into his arms, sobbing their names; ignoring whatever it was they were trying to tell him through their chattering teeth; ignoring the dog, Lady, who barked and leapt around and shook her sopping coat all over everyone.

It was Andy who eventually explained what had happened, when he'd gotten the children inside and calmed the dog. Andy and the Halperts, an elderly couple Max hadn't even noticed standing there on the porch with the others.

He knew them slightly, the way he knew everyone in Newberry Cove. They had always seemed friendly. Not today.

Today, they wore accusatory expressions as they perched on his sagging sofa and told him how his children had been drifting in the water on a makeshift raft and how a stranger, a woman, had dived in to rescue them when they got into trouble.

Even Andy—jovial, easygoing Andy—seemed disapproving as he asked Max how the children had managed to sneak away.

What could Max do but admit that he must have fallen asleep?

He couldn't tell them that he'd been exhausted for so long—his nights tormented by nightmares, his days filled with caring for the children and single-handedly doing the necessary construction to make this old shingled cottage livable year-round.

No, telling them that wouldn't make a difference. They wouldn't easily forgive him for what he had done.

Nor would he forgive himself. Ever.

Now, as he lay in his small bed in the minuscule master bedroom, reliving the whole near-tragedy, he allowed himself to wonder, for the first time, who she had been— the woman who had saved his beloved children.

He should find her. Thank her. Maybe reward her.

Wasn't that what people did for Good Samaritans?

But what could he possibly pay in return for the priceless gift she had given him?

He sighed in the dark, listening to their even breathing from the sleeping loft above the living room. He'd left his door open tonight just so he could hear them breathe,

knowing the sound would comfort him, reassure him that
they were going to be all right.

The only thing was, if he had slipped up this once,
couldn't it happen again?

No, he would never allow himself to fall asleep again
while he was supervising them. No matter how tired he
was, he would drink gallons of coffee; he wouldn't go
near his easy chair; he would never again dare to rest
until the children were safely tucked into their little beds
at night.

And they sure as hell would never venture out onto
the water again; they had given their word on that. They
were still shell-shocked from what had happened, reliving
their near-drowning repeatedly, forcing Max to mask his
own gut-wrenching horror each time, lest they dwell on
it indefinitely. What mattered was that they were safe and
they had learned their lesson.

But next time, it might be something else. Some other
danger that would rise up to threaten their safety. The
world was a precarious place, and for all the tragedies in
his past, Max had never felt as vulnerable—as alone—as
he did now.

Too bad there really is no such thing as guardian angels, he
thought as he rolled over onto his side and stared bleakly
into space.

TWO

Olivia rarely read the weekly local paper, the *Newberry News*. But business was slow at the veterinary clinic the stormy Saturday morning that followed her rescue of the two children from the water and she found herself straightening the piles of magazines and newspapers in Dr. Klimek's waiting room just for something to do.

It wasn't a front-page headline.

No, that belonged to the three-alarm fire that had flattened Paul McCutcheon's barn on Halloween night.

The item about the rescue was relegated to the second page, alongside a wire story about the Middle East peace conference. Apparently, in typical small-town fashion, local news was at least as important as international, if not more so.

MYSTERY WOMAN RESCUES
DROWNING TYKES

The headline caught Olivia's eye, and her heart sank as she scanned the article that followed.

What started as a mischievous caper nearly ended in tragedy for two local children on Wednesday afternoon. Six-year-old Lindsey and Sam Rothwell, twin son and daughter of Max Rothwell, Newberry's former mayor, would surely have met a dire fate if not for the efforts of an elusive woman who appeared out of nowhere to save their lives.

The Rothwell children were on board a makeshift raft when it capsized, tossing them into the water. According to eyewitnesses Harold and Marge Halpert, the woman, a jogger, raced across the beach and plunged into the frigid water to rescue the children. She was able to get them both to shore, where she administered CPR to Lindsey, who had stopped breathing. By the time the Halperts were able to reach the scene, the woman, described as a slender brunette, had vanished.

"It was as if she were a guardian angel," Marge Halpert told this reporter.

"An undercover angel," her husband Harold added. "That woman obviously didn't want to stick around and take credit for what she did."

The Rothwell children also insist that their savior was an angel.

"She was beautiful—she looked just like my mommy," young Lindsey Rothwell told the Halperts, who brought the children to the Newberry police department after the incident.

The children's mother, Julia Samuelson Rothwell, tragically died in an automobile accident shortly after their birth. They live outside of town with their father Max, who is well-known in this area as Newberry's longtime mayor, having served several terms in office before abruptly resigning after his wife's death. His father, Jack Rothwell, preceded him in that post, serving as Newberry's mayor from the early 1950s until his death nearly a decade ago.

The children were in Max Rothwell's care at the time of the incident. Mr. Rothwell declined to comment for this article.

Meanwhile, the people of Newberry can rest assured that there is apparently an angel in their midst.

"Oh, my God," Olivia breathed softly, setting the paper down on a table and turning toward the window.

She could see T.J. and Dr. Klimek in the parking area, walking a dog whose leg had recently been amputated. The animal limped along gamely on his remaining three legs. T.J., dressed snugly in his Polar fleece jacket and cap, walked backward in front of the doctor and the dog, coaxing the animal onward.

He's happy here, Olivia thought, seeing the unabashed grin on her son's face. *This is home to him. How can I take him away?*

She sank wearily into a chair, rubbing her forehead and trying to think clearly.

So she had rescued two children and the locals were talking. So what?

That didn't mean she'd blown her cover. It didn't mean she had to pick up and move again, leaving everything behind and vanishing in the middle of the night as she had before.

She might have called some unwanted attention to herself, but that didn't mean anybody knew her real identity. In fact, they didn't even know who she was pretending to be.

Mystery Woman, the paper had called her.

What if somebody figured out that the mystery woman—the so-called undercover angel—was Olivia Halloran, a single mom who lived in a rundown farmhouse on the outskirts of town and kept to herself?

That didn't mean the news was going to hit the A.P. wire service, did it? It didn't mean that her face—her new face—was going to be splashed everywhere from here to the West Coast.

It didn't mean *he* would see her. That he would come after her and T.J. and—

No. God, no.

But there was always a chance, wasn't there? Always a nagging *what-if* . . .

Olivia closed her eyes and thought back to that day, more than three years ago, when she and T.J. had stopped at the supermarket in the tiny midwestern town where they'd been living. They had been laughing, singing some silly song, as she loaded the cart with things they needed.

Peanut butter.

Bread.

Milk.

A carton of milk.

She froze as she started to put the milk into the shopping cart, gasped involuntarily as she stared at the face looking back at her.

T.J.'s face.

Though the image had been taken from an old photograph when he was barely a toddler, the face had been altered to show what he might look like a year or two later. It couldn't have been more accurate.

The picture looked just like him.

Above his face was the word *MISSING.*

Olivia had flung the carton back into the dairy case, taken T.J. from the cart, and hurried from the store. She had driven away from that town without even going back to the small apartment they were renting. They'd left everything behind once again.

T.J. wasn't even three years old then. Too young to be seriously affected by the sudden move.

But he had been living here in Newberry for several years now. For all she knew, he had no memory of that tiny midwestern town, and he certainly didn't know about California. They rarely talked about the past.

Only when he asked, as he did more and more frequently, about his father.

She had told him the truth: that his daddy had died. She hadn't told him where, or how. And she tried to answer his questions as truthfully as she could. Tried not to betray her own emotions.

That wouldn't be fair. T.J. didn't need to know what had happened. Not for a long, long time—if ever.

She glanced out the window again and saw Dr. Klimek, his back to her in his red-and-black plaid wool jacket, crouch down beside T.J. to tell him something.

The elderly doctor was the only friend they had here. He wasn't like the rest of them, the close-knit residents of Newberry. He kept to himself, and that made him almost as much an outsider as Olivia and T.J. were, though she suspected he had lived here all his life.

He wasn't much of a conversationalist, and to her relief, he had never asked her about her past, just as she didn't ask about his. She didn't know whether he had ever been married, and she doubted he had children.

Nobody ever seemed to come around him, except, of course, for his customers. He was the only veterinarian in the area, and he was an excellent one, at that. He seemed to have a knack for communicating with animals that he lacked for communicating with humans. Except T.J.

Olivia's son had recently developed an affinity for her elderly boss, and the man, though a loner, had reciprocated.

After school and on Saturdays, T.J. spent time at the clinic, helping the doctor with minor tasks. She had no idea what they talked about when they spent time together, but assumed it was simply the animals they both loved. T.J. had already declared that he wanted to be a vet when he grew up.

Olivia, meanwhile, enjoyed her work at the clinic; but being a veterinary technician was hardly what she would have chosen for herself. She had been a real people-person, once upon a time. She might have done well in sales or politics or perhaps social work.

Then Thomas had come along, and she'd never had the chance to pursue anything other than marriage and motherhood.

Now there was just motherhood. Just taking care of her son—and collecting the weekly pay from Dr. Klimek. He gave it to her in cash. They both preferred it that way—under the table. The old veterinarian had said he didn't have the patience for the paperwork the government demanded for on-the-books employees.

Her salary wasn't much, but it allowed her to put food on the table and pay the rent on the ancient farmhouse she was leasing on a dirt road outside of town.

The owner, who had inherited the place from his mother, lived in New York City; Olivia sent her money order faithfully once a month, and he left her alone. Whenever something had to be fixed around the house, Olivia did it herself. She didn't always know what she was doing, but anything was better than having the owner, or worse, a local electrician or plumber, come snooping around the place.

Olivia heard the sound of tires crunching on the gravel drive outside, then car doors slamming in the parking area just beyond view of the window. She saw Dr. Klimek and T.J. heading in that direction and assumed a new patient had been brought in.

She glanced at the newspaper she'd put down before, then, after consideration, snatched it up and carried it over to the blue recycling bin in the corner. She put the paper inside, burying it beneath several old issues of *Popular Mechanics*.

Moments later, the door opened.

Olivia looked up.

Her jaw dropped.

"It's her!"

Startled, Max Rothwell glanced from Sam to Lindsey, who had spoken simultaneously. He had no idea what their outburst meant, but saw that they were both staring at the only occupant of the waiting area of the veterinarian's office and that they apparently recognized her.

He, too, stared—though not for the same reason.

He had never seen her before; he would have remembered. Not only was she beautiful, but there was a striking vulnerability about her. The look in her big dark eyes was haunting, as though she had been caught off guard, unwillingly captured in a spotlight's glare.

He noted the wavy brown hair that fell below her shoulders; the high cheekbones; the body so slender it was clearly all angles beneath the bulky Nordic sweater and jeans she wore. She was fragile and remote, and there was something about her that made him want to help.

"It's her, Daddy," Sam said, tugging his jacket.

"The angel," Lindsey breathed in awe.

And he knew, then, that this was the woman who had rescued his children.

So shocked was he that he had somehow, unexpectedly, come face-to-face with her, that he was speechless.

How could this be?

If Andy hadn't convinced him to take a puppy from his dog's litter to give to Sam and Lindsey . . .

If he hadn't needed to get the dog the necessary shots . . .

If Dr. Klimek hadn't been the only vet listed in the local yellow pages . . .

He might never have known who she was, the "Mystery Woman" his children assumed could only be celestial.

He could only stare at her now as she gaped at his children, not even seeming to have noticed him yet.

Then Lindsey said, "This is our Daddy," and the woman's gaze shifted to his face.

She looked . . . not reluctant.

Not embarrassed or awkward or shy, all reactions he might have expected, under the circumstances.

No, the expression she wore was something else, something he couldn't define until he saw her take a step away from him. Yes, she had backed away, a subtle gesture but one he hadn't missed, and that was when he realized that the expression etched across her lovely face was fear.

She was afraid.

Of what?

Of *him?*

Of his *children?*

It made no sense. Yet there was no denying her expression, or the wary stance she had taken.

The door opened again behind him. In stepped the old veterinarian he'd spoken with outside in the parking lot, along with the boy, who was now carrying the three-legged hound.

"Hey, Mom, did you see him walk out there? I was helping him!" the boy exclaimed, bounding across the room to the woman, who still stood frozen, so obviously afraid.

"All right, Mr. Rothwell," the old man said briskly, heading toward a door that apparently led to an examining room. "Let's take care of your dog. Olivia, please come with us to assist."

"What about the kids?" Max asked, tearing his attention from the mystery woman.

"They can wait here with T.J. Too many people in the examining room makes the animals nervous."

"I don't know . . ." Max said, hesitant, looking at the children.

He sensed the same note of concern in Olivia's expression when he glanced at her. She was worriedly watching her son.

"They'll be fine," Dr. Klimek said in a brusque, nononsense tone, clearly for both their benefit. "I'll leave the door open so you can see them from the other room."

"All right," Max agreed, and turned to Sam and Lindsey. "You two stay right here, do you hear me? And don't get into anything. I'll take Lady in while the doctor gives her the shots."

"Okay, Daddy," Lindsey said.

Sam was already standing near the other little boy, T.J., petting the maimed dog he still cradled.

"T.J., behave yourself, okay?" the woman said softly.

The doctor had called her *Olivia*.

The name didn't seem to suit her.

Max wasn't quite sure why. He just didn't see her as an Olivia.

Some people had names that seemed to perfectly reflect who they were.

Julia, for instance, had been classically beautiful, sophisticated, regal. Max's father, Jack, had been jovial and easygoing.

Max wasn't sure what an *Olivia* was supposed to look like, but this woman simply wasn't it.

"I'll be back in a few minutes. I'm right in there if you need me," Max told his children.

"You're going with the angel, Daddy. She'll take care of you and Lady," Lindsey piped up as he patted her on the head.

Dr. Klimek, who had already disappeared through the door, didn't seem to have heard the comment.

But the woman, Olivia, had. Max saw her stiffen. Again, his gaze met hers; again, he saw fear there.

He didn't know whether to acknowledge his daughter's comment and ask her about the rescue or simply let it be. He sensed that, for whatever reason, she would prefer that he ignore his children's recognition of her. Maybe that would be best.

For now.

He followed her into the next room, bringing Lady along by pulling her collar. The dog didn't have a leash. Max hadn't had a chance to buy one yet, and there seemed to be little reason, considering that they lived in the middle of nowhere.

The doctor had changed into a white coat. Now Olivia did, too, pulling it on over her sweater. It was too big for her, and she rolled up the sleeves, revealing bony forearms. Again, Max was struck by her delicate vulnerability and found himself wondering about that.

According to his children and the Halperts, she had single-handedly dragged Sam, Lindsey, and the raft through frigid waves, then had resuscitated Lindsey on the beach before sprinting away, seemingly unburdened by her drenched clothes or the icy wind.

He had pictured their rescuer as a robust, outdoorsy type—not this fragile, ethereal beauty.

"Please hold the dog, Olivia," the doctor said briskly after lifting Lady onto the table.

"What's her name?" she asked, addressing Max directly for the first time, though she didn't look at him.

"It's Lady."

"There, now, Lady," she soothed in the dog's ear, smoothing her furry head. "It's going to be all right."

The doctor pulled out a syringe.

He immunized the dog with Olivia's assistance as Max watched.

He noted the woman's gentle touch, her soothing voice, the way she constantly reassured the frightened, trembling animal.

He found himself wondering, for some insane reason, what it would be like to have her stroke his head that way, to hear her murmuring those comforting words in his ear.

You're out of your mind, Rothwell, he told himself, and tried to snap out of it.

But he couldn't seem to help himself. There was something about her, something intriguing and alluring, and he had a feeling he wouldn't soon forget her after they parted company this afternoon.

All too soon, the doctor was finished with Lady.

Max followed him and Olivia back into the waiting room, the dog trotting contentedly beside Olivia, gazing up at her as though she were a newfound mistress.

"She likes you," Max told her gruffly as the doctor stepped behind the counter to mark something in the file he'd created for Lady.

Olivia merely smiled faintly and turned her attention to her son, who was deep in conversations with Sam and Lindsey. The three seemed to have become fast friends in the fifteen minutes or so that they had been left alone.

Now, as Max told his twins to get their coats on, Lindsey asked, "Can T.J. come over to play with us, Daddy?"

"Yeah, can he?" Sam echoed.

"Can I, Mom?" T.J. joined in.

Max didn't miss the look of dismay in Olivia's eyes and was sure that it was mirrored in his own. He didn't want his children to play with her son.

He didn't want that because . . .

Why didn't he want that?

Because.

If T.J. came over to play, it would mean he would be forced to see T.J.'s mother again. He didn't want that.

No, the last thing he needed was to be distracted by a beautiful woman.

He had his hands full just raising his children and turning the cottage into a decent home for all of them. The need for sleep was distracting enough; look what had happened just the other day when he'd closed his eyes for just a moment. He'd nearly lost his children.

He knew that getting entangled with a woman like Olivia whoever-she-was would be far more exhausting than anything else he'd undertaken.

Look at the way Julia had drained him in their short years together.

He had sworn, after she died, never to fall in love again. No matter how lonely he became, no matter how much he desired a woman . . . he would never allow himself to give to anyone—besides his children—what he had tried to give to Julia.

Julia had taken all he had to offer, and then some.

But all women aren't Julia, a small voice protested in his mind as he stared at Olivia, who was standing with her hands on her son's shoulders in a protective maternal pose.

Not all women were complicated and demanding and self-centered.

Though she was a stranger, he couldn't imagine Olivia treating him as Julia had.

Then again, he knew—despite the fact that she was a stranger—that Olivia was hardly an uncomplicated woman.

He had seen the fear in her eyes when she gazed at him. He knew she had something to hide.

Whatever it was, *whoever* she was, didn't matter.

"Can T.J. come over, Daddy?" Lindsey asked again, tugging the hem of his jacket.

Helpless, he looked at Olivia.

He knew that it wouldn't matter what he said. He saw in her eyes that, for whatever reason, she had no intention of allowing her son to play with his children.

"Sometime, sure," he said, feeling safe with the response and gratified by the happy grins on all three children's faces.

"When can I, Mom?" T.J. asked Olivia.

"We'll see," she said vaguely, avoiding his gaze—and Max's, too.

"Mr. Rothwell?" Dr. Klimek called.

As Max wrote a check and thanked the veterinarian, he was aware that Olivia was watching him. He realized he owed her his gratitude as well—not just for helping calm Lady just now, but for saving his children's lives. He might not want to become entangled with her in any way, yet he could hardly leave this office without acknowledging what she had done.

But when he turned around again, she was disappearing into an examining room without a backward glance.

It's just as well, he told himself as he got the children and the dog together and headed out into the blustery day.

T.J. talked of nothing but Sam and Lindsey as Olivia warmed a can of tomato soup and put together a couple of grilled-cheese-and-bacon sandwiches for dinner that night.

He told Olivia things she already knew—that their mother was dead and that they were twins—and things she didn't. Like, they weren't allowed to go to school because their father insisted on teaching them at home and their father said they would never have a new mommy, even though they kept asking for one.

It was surprising that a man who looked like Max Rothwell hadn't remarried by now and that he didn't intend to.

She had done her best not to notice his looks, but couldn't help it.

The man was blatantly gorgeous. He was tall, with a rugged, broad-shouldered build that appeared to be solid muscle beneath the blue jeans and flannel shirt he wore. His eyes, fringed by lush, dark lashes, were a deep gray-blue, the precise hue of shadows falling across fresh snow late on a winter afternoon. He had full lips, even white teeth, a strong jawline. The one imperfect feature on his face was his nose, which was slightly crooked, as though it had been broken years ago. But it didn't mar his appearance; rather, it gave him character, made him human.

So why, with all his rugged, sexy appeal, was Max Rothwell living alone? Why hadn't he found a willing stepmother for his two adorable children?

It's none of my business, Olivia told herself.

And she didn't intend to make anything about the Rothwells her business, despite T.J.'s apparent obsession with them. She had never seen him as animated as he'd been this afternoon when shed found the three children chatting in the waiting room after Lady had been tended to.

She felt a twinge of guilt, knowing she would never allow him to make Sam and Lindsey his playmates.

It hurt her to think that her son's only friend was an aging veterinarian.

She fleetingly thought back to her own childhood, to the dozens of friends and neighbors who had populated her happy-go-lucky existence. Though she'd been an only child, she had never been lonely.

Not that T.J. had ever complained of being lonely.

In fact, she hadn't really paid much attention, until now, to the fact that he didn't seem to talk about any of the children at school. Not once since he'd enrolled in kindergarten two months ago had he mentioned a particular classmate or asked to play at someone's house or have a friend over.

Olivia pondered this as she poured the soup into bowls and carried them to the slightly wobbly Formica-topped table in the drafty kitchen. Luckily, the house had come furnished, and what was there was adequate, if not particularly modern or attractive. The appliances were functional, and there was even a color television and stereo in the threadbare living room.

The kitchen lacked a dishwasher, but it wasn't as though Olivia and T.J. generated many dirty dishes. Now, as she set the soup bowls on the table beside the two sandwich plates and milk-filled glasses, she found herself feeling hollow inside.

For the first time, she wondered how it was going to affect T.J., growing up in this isolated world she'd created, with nobody but her in his life.

For so long, she'd focused on being grateful that they had each other; that they'd escaped the nightmares of the past. Now she swallowed over a lump in her throat as she gazed at her son, who obediently slid into his chair across from hers.

"Do you ever feel lonely, T.J.?" she asked reluctantly as she sat down with him.

"Lonely? Sometimes. I wish I had a twin, like Sam and Lindsey do," he said wistfully. "Or even just a brother or sister."

"I used to wish for a brother or sister sometimes, too," Olivia lied.

The truth was, she'd always been content. Her parents

had showered her with attention; she had had tons of friends, and when she got older, plenty of boyfriends. She couldn't recall ever feeling alone . . . until she married Thomas.

Quickly, she shoved the chilling thought of him from her mind and stirred her thick red soup with her spoon, making clinking noises against the edge of the wide bowl.

"What's wrong, Mom?" T.J. asked.

She looked up to see him watching her solemnly.

"Nothing."

"Do you want to get married again so that you can have more babies?"

She dropped her spoon and it slid into the soup.

"No, I don't want to get married again," she said, wincing as she burned her fingers fishing out the spoon. She wiped the sticky handle on a paper napkin, then looked up at her son. "Why do you ask?"

"I just thought maybe you could marry Sam and Lindsey's daddy, even though he doesn't want a wife. Then I would have a brother and a sister."

"T.J.—" Olivia broke off, stopping to carefully consider her response. "I know you think it would be fun to have a big family. Sometimes I think so, too. But right now, it doesn't look like that's going to happen. I'm happy the way things are—aren't you? I get to give all my attention to you. You don't have to share me with anyone." She ruffled his hair. "And I don't have to share you, either."

He shrugged and picked up his sandwich. "I wouldn't mind sharing," he mumbled around a bite. "Mrs. Starkey said you're s'posed to share. Sharing's good."

Knowing better than to argue with the wisdom of a kindergarten teacher, Olivia said only, "Sharing *is* good. But it's not always necessary."

"Well, if Sam and Lindsey can't be my brother and sister, they can still be my friends, right?"

Olivia sipped her soup, her stomach churning as it went down.

"Right, Mom?" he persisted.

She set down her spoon. "I don't know, T.J."

"What don't you know?"

"It's not as if we'll be seeing a lot of them. You're busy with school, and I'm busy with work—"

"Not all the time!" he protested. "I have time for playing."

"That's true. But they don't live nearby. Don't you think it's better to make friends with children in our own neighborhood?"

"What neighborhood?"

He had a point. Olivia had deliberately chosen to rent a house on a road where other homes were few and far between, the better to hold the world at bay.

Now, though, it was becoming apparent that she couldn't keep T.J. in a cage forever. The older he got, the more freedom he was going to demand. Sooner or later, he'd realize that they didn't even have a telephone, which he hadn't missed until now. She hadn't bothered to have one hooked up. Why bother?

But someday, T.J. would notice, and he'd want one.

Besides, she wanted him to make friends—to live a normal childhood. Wasn't that why she'd run away with him in the first place?

Well, that was part of the reason.

You did it to save your life, too, she reminded herself. *Don't ever forget it. Don't ever let your guard down, not even for a moment.*

"We'll talk later about seeing Sam and Lindsey, okay, T.J.?" she said.

He brightened, and she tried to ignore the guilt that jabbed her. She *did* want him to make friends, but she had no intention of letting him see the Rothwell children again.

It wasn't just that she had rescued them from the water and stirred up all kinds of local attention and gossip about a mystery woman—though that was reason enough to stay away.

Max Rothwell . . .

Well, he was an even better reason.

She couldn't see him again.

Seeing a man like that made her want things that she could never have.

Things he obviously didn't want, either.

Why didn't he want to remarry?

He must have his reasons. So do you.

And that, she told herself firmly, *is that.*

THREE

Two weeks had passed since Max had brought Lady to Dr. Klimek's office. Two whole weeks, and every single day, Max found himself thinking about Olivia.

He hadn't thanked her.

Why hadn't he thanked her for what she had done? He had promised himself, before he happened to stumble across her, that he would track down the woman who had rescued his children; that he would thank her, even reward her.

But when she unexpectedly was there, in front of him, he hadn't so much as mentioned the incident.

Surely she knew *he* knew what she had done.

Not only had the children told him she was their mysterious angel, but news of the rescue had been in the paper for the whole damn town to see.

Everyone in Newberry Cove knew that Max Rothwell had fallen asleep while he was supposed to be watching his kids and that the kids had found their way out onto the water and nearly drowned. Everyone knew that a woman had pulled them out.

What nobody seemed to know was who the woman was.

Even now that Max knew where to find her—at the animal clinic—he had no idea who she was. A few years ago, when he was mayor of Newberry Cove, he had known every single citizen of the town and most families in the surrounding rural areas. Why didn't he know her?

Obviously, she had come here within the past few years.

But few people moved to this remote area of coastal Maine that was so far from the touristy areas. It was unheard of for a young, single mother to settle here.

He knew she was single because Sam and Lindsey had told him that.

They'd told him because he'd asked.

"Does T.J. have a daddy?" he'd found himself inquiring as he drove them home from the clinic that afternoon— even as he asked himself, irritated, *Why do you want to know?*

Why had he been so relieved when his children had said T.J. only had a mommy?

Why was he so interested in the other details they related in their childish innocence, details gleaned from a candid conversation among six-year-olds?

He found out that T.J. and his mommy lived in a farmhouse on a dirt road not far from the veterinarian's office; that they had lived here for a few years, and that T.J. was in kindergarten in the Newberry Cove elementary school.

That didn't explain what Olivia was doing here, or why he had glimpsed stark fear in her eyes when his children had recognized her as their "angel."

And it didn't explain who she was or why he didn't know her already.

Was it because he had, in the years since he'd been the local mayor, removed himself as completely from Newberry Cove as was possible without physically leaving the area?

Or was it because she didn't *want* to be known?

He'd been toying with that idea on and off for the past few weeks.

Why else would she have taken off after rescuing the kids—running off down the beach, according to Marge

Halpert, "as though the hounds of hell were nipping her heels"?

Why else would she have been afraid when the kids had recognized her in Doctor Klimek's office?

Why else would she have hesitated to agree to a play date between T.J. and the twins?

You were reluctant, too, Max reminded himself now as he steered his green Ford Explorer over the rutted lane leading away from his cabin.

But his reluctance stemmed from an unwillingness to expose himself—and his long-dormant libido—to T.J.'s beautiful mother.

What was *her* story?

It could be the same thing.

She might have sensed the flicker of attraction between them. She might want to avoid it as much as he did.

In fact, she must have sensed it. How could she have missed it? It was about as easy to ignore as a blizzard on the Fourth of July.

And she must want to avoid it. She hadn't flirted with him, the way most single, available women did on the rare occasions when he ventured out in public.

She hadn't slipped him her phone number or shown up at his door or made any other overture to suggest that she was interested in him.

So she isn't looking for a man.

That alone was enough to set her apart from the few single women in these parts—all of whom had grown up here and chosen to stay for whatever reason.

Like Mary Pratt, who had gone off to medical school in Boston, then moved back to Newberry Cove so that she could commute to work at a Bangor hospital while caring for her aging parents.

And Sheila O'Connor, who had taken over her father's large, profitable tree farm when he passed away.

Max had grown up with both Mary and Sheila. He had dated both of them before Julia slammed into his life, knocking the wind right out of him. By the time he knew what had hit him, he was married.

Unhappily so.

And he never intended to take a chance on that happening again.

So anything more than a passing acquaintance with Olivia—he didn't even know her last name—was out of the question.

He knew it, and he suspected she wanted it the same way.

That was why he was headed for Dr. Klimek's office on this cold, rainy afternoon.

He'd left the twins at home with Sarah Polucci, his friend Andy's mother, who stopped by every so often with a tray of homemade lasagna and strict orders for him to make himself scarce while she gave the place a good cleaning.

He had protested this habit of hers on many occasions before Andy finally convinced him that there was no stopping her and he should know that by now.

Sarah Polucci had treated Max like a second son after his own mother had died early in his childhood.

Only when he married Julia did she stop coming around, and that, he knew, was because she didn't like his bride. The feeling was mutual.

Julia had called Sarah a fat old busybody—not to her face, but that was beside the point. She had made it clear in her attitude from the moment Max introduced the two women. He had been hoping Sarah could be a kind of surrogate mother-in-law for his wife. He had hoped a lot of things that hadn't happened.

It wasn't until Julia was gone that Sarah started coming

around again, taking care of the young widower and his infant twins as though they were her own grandchildren.

Sam and Lindsey loved her, and whenever she showed up, they joined Sarah in urging Max to clear out of the house. He always used the time to run errands in town, and when he returned home, he invariably found the house sparkling and the three of them playing Go Fish or Chutes and Ladders at the kitchen table.

Today, however, Max wasn't using his free time to run the usual local errands—grocery shopping, bill paying, that sort of thing.

No, today, he was headed for Dr. Klimek's office.

He was going to find Olivia and he was going to thank her.

He was even, God help him, going to invite her son T.J. over for a play date, if she agreed to it.

Sam and Lindsey had been pestering him to do just that, and he had come to realize that he couldn't keep them from making friends for the rest of their lives.

As it was, he was home-schooling them and raising them in the middle of nowhere. But just because he didn't want anything to do with the rest of the world didn't mean they should suffer. They had each other, it was true—but that didn't mean they couldn't make friends with other children.

As long as it didn't lead to some kind of whirlwind social life—and it wouldn't. Not with T.J.

Max was sure of that. If his instincts were on target, T.J.'s mother wasn't the type to try and drag him—and his children—back to civilization. She wouldn't ask nosy questions or pry, and she clearly wasn't a part of the local gossip mill since she had managed to keep her existence under wraps for this long. If Harold and Marge Halpert didn't recognize her, she kept to herself.

And since she so clearly wasn't interested in Max, there wasn't even that obstacle to worry about.

He had concluded that the fact that sparks had flown between them on their first encounter wasn't reason enough for him to stay away.

He at least owed her a proper thank you.

As he pulled into the clinic parking lot, he was dismayed to see that it was empty except for a battered red pickup truck. He couldn't imagine Olivia driving a vehicle like that. It must belong to the old man.

Sure enough, when he stepped inside the waiting room, he saw that Dr. Klimek was the lone occupant. He was seated behind the desk, holding a small, malnourished-looking kitten.

"Mr. Rothwell," he said when Max walked in.

"Hello, Dr. Klimek."

Max had known the doctor all his life, the way he knew most people in the area. But Dr. Klimek was a loner, and always had been.

And since Max had never had a pet until now, he had never found it necessary to venture into the veterinarian's office.

Therefore, he didn't feel entirely comfortable now as he tried to think of a way to ask about Olivia without seeming . . . well, nosy.

"What can I do for you today?" the old man asked, gently setting the kitten into a nearby cushioned basket. "Is Lady all right?"

Impressed that the vet remembered his dog's name, Max nodded. "Lady's fine."

He cleared his throat.

The doctor waited.

"I was just wondering . . ." Max hesitated. The man's unflinching stare wasn't making this any easier. "The woman who works here . . . Olivia, is it?"

Dr. Klimek nodded.

"I don't suppose she's here today?"

"No," came the terse reply.

Not: *"She doesn't work on Mondays."*

Not: *"She quit her job last week and moved away."*

Not: *"She's home with a terrible head cold."*

Just . . . *no.*

This wasn't going to be an easy conversation.

"Well," Max said, struggling for a casual tone, "I need to get in touch with her. Would you mind giving me her phone number, Dr. Klimek?"

"I can't."

Taken aback even though he'd anticipated a less-than-forthcoming response, Max said, "Could you at least tell me her last name so that I can look it up?"

"She doesn't have a telephone."

Max blinked. "Oh."

There was silence as Dr. Klimek waited for him to say something else. No wonder the man always kept to himself. His social skills left something to be desired.

"Could you . . . would you mind telling me where she lives so that I can stop by and talk to her, then?" Max asked.

"I can't do that, either."

"But . . . why not?"

"It wouldn't be right. It would be violating Olivia's privacy."

"I see."

Max wondered if it was the very private Dr. Klimek who was worried about Olivia's privacy, or Olivia herself. Why didn't she have a phone? Even Max had a phone, though he rarely used it. It seemed necessary, in case of an emergency, when you lived so far from town with two young children.

He knew that Olivia, too, lived on a rural road, thanks to the information her son had given the twins. But that didn't mean that he could find her. There were hundreds of old farmhouses on hundreds of dirt roads in the area.

What could he do but thank Dr. Klimek—*for nothing,* he thought grimly—and turn to leave?

It wasn't until he was about to open the door and venture back out into the rain that an idea struck him.

He turned back.

The veterinarian had once again picked up the scruffy little kitten and was cradling the animal so tenderly in his arms that Max instantly forgave him his aloofness.

"Yes?" Dr. Klimek asked, looking up at him expectantly.

"I just wondered . . . if I wrote a note to Olivia, would you see that she gets it?"

The man hesitated.

"I promise it's perfectly respectable. You can read it if you like."

"That won't be necessary," Dr. Klimek said.

Max fought back a smile, knowing that a man who was so big on privacy would never read something addressed to someone else.

He borrowed a pen and paper and forced himself to scrawl a quick note when he wanted to think it through carefully. That just wasn't possible; not with the old man watching him warily.

Dear Olivia,

When we met two weeks ago, I'm afraid I neglected to thank you for rescuing my children. Please know that I will always be grateful for what you did and that, if there's any way I can repay you, I fully intend to do so. Sam and Lindsey would like to invite T.J. over to play one afternoon next week. I would be happy to pick him up and drop him off again afterward. Please call me at 555-9184 to make arrangements.

Sincerely,
Max Rothwell

He folded the note and handed it to Dr. Klimek along with the pen.

"I'd appreciate your giving this to her," he said.

The man nodded and carefully tucked the folded paper beneath a glass paperweight on the desk.

"Thank you.

Dr. Klimek nodded.

Max started to walk away.

"Just so you know," he said, as an afterthought, turning back to Dr. Klimek again when he reached the door, "I'm not interested in her. Romantically, I mean. It's my kids . . . They want to be friends with T.J."

Was he mistaken or was there a flicker of a smile in Dr. Klimek's gray eyes, just for a fleeting moment?

It was hard to tell.

There was no sign of humor now, just the same expressionless features as always.

And if a smile *had* actually been there, Max had no idea what it meant.

Did the doctor think he was lying about not being interested in Olivia?

Because I'm not, he thought defensively as he went back out into the rain and wind.

All I wanted to do was thank her and extend an invitation. To her son, not to her.

Olivia was a desirable woman, but Max didn't desire her.

No, that wasn't quite true.

He desired her, but he wouldn't let his desire get any further than his own mind. He couldn't get hurt by secretly lusting after an attractive stranger.

Anything more than that would be dangerous.

It was a mistake to come here, he told himself with a sinking heart as he got behind the wheel and started the Explorer.

For a moment, he considered dashing back inside and asking Dr. Klimek to rip up the note.

If he did that, he wondered if the veterinarian would still mention to Olivia that he had been here asking about her.

Somehow, he couldn't imagine Dr. Klimek offering anyone information about anything without being asked, and not even then.

If he took the note back, then she would never know.

But if he took the note back, *he* would never know how she might have responded.

His mind made up, he jerked the car into gear and drove out of the parking lot.

The local elementary school was a red brick building with white-paned windows and a spindly white wooden bell tower on top—the kind of building one might expect to house a school in a small New England town.

Olivia hurried along the empty corridor toward the kindergarten classroom, where Mrs. Starkey, T.J.'s teacher, was waiting for her.

Moments ago she'd left T.J. in the principal's office under the watchful eye of the school secretary, Mrs. Randall, who had assured her that he would be just fine. The woman had given him some crayons and sheets of paper, and he was happily occupied, "safe and sound," as the secretary had pointed out.

Of course, she had no idea what Olivia and T.J. had been through or how difficult it was for her to leave her son in that office under these circumstances.

She would much rather have brought him with her to this meeting to which the teacher had summoned her, but Mrs. Starkey wanted to speak privately. Not wanting to seem overprotective, Olivia had agreed.

Now, her heart pounded in time with her heels tapping on the wooden floor as she made her way to the classroom.

Her instincts told her to run in the opposite direction. Just go and grab T.J. and run.

She knows, she told herself, fighting back panic.

She knows.

She's waiting in there with the police, and they're going to take me away and lock me up forever . . .

"Mrs. Halloran?"

There was Mrs. Starkey, poking her head out into the hallway. It was too late to run.

There was nowhere to hide.

"Hello," Olivia heard her voice say.

"How have you been?" the teacher asked, a warm smile on her pudgy, middle-aged face; and in that instant, Olivia allowed herself to relax, just a little.

Mrs. Starkey wouldn't be wearing that friendly smile if she were about to turn Olivia over to the authorities, would she?

Unless it was a trap.

"Come on in," Mrs. Starkey said, holding the classroom door open and stepping aside.

Olivia hesitated.

Then, because there was nothing to do but obey the invitation that felt more like a command, she made herself move forward.

As she stepped into the classroom, a wave of nostalgic longing washed over her. She took in the small tables and chairs, green chalkboards, alphabet borders, crayoned drawings on manila paper; inhaled the air that smelled faintly of chalk dust and milk; heard the steam heat hissing and the raindrops pattering on the wide glass windows.

This was a safe, cozy little nest, like one she had inhab-

ited in her long-ago other life. She remembered being
in grade school, playing jacks and trading lunch-box sandwiches with her friends, skipping home to tell her mother
all about her day.

Was that the last time she had ever felt safe?

Of course not.

But it had been so long since she had allowed herself
to think back on her childhood, on anything that had
happened before she had arrived in Newberry Cove.

Was T.J. as content in this classroom as she had been
in her own? Was she somehow, despite her doubts, man-
aging to give him the kind of normal, healthy childhood
she'd had?

Her momentary reassurance that that might be the case
was dashed by Mrs. Starkey's next words.

"Have a seat, please, Mrs. Halloran. I have a dentist's
appointment in a half hour so I'm not going to beat
around the bush here. I'd like to talk to you about a
problem T.J. has been having lately—really, since the
school year began."

Olivia's heart sank as she lowered herself into the only
adult-size wooden chair in the room, beside the teacher's
desk.

"What kind of problem?"

"Don't look so alarmed, Mrs. Halloran . . ."

Olivia noted the *Mrs.* the teacher had attached to her
name.

She just assumes, Olivia told herself, marveling at that
even as she acknowledged that even in this day and age,
the families of a small New England town like Newberry
Cove were mainly traditional. A father, a mother, and several happy children.

She opened her mouth to correct Mrs. Starkey, to say
that it was Ms. Halloran, but stopped herself. That might
mean offering an explanation as to where T.J.'s father

was, and the last thing she wanted to do was talk about him.

You could always make something up, she reminded herself.

But there are too many lies already, she thought wearily, and remained silent.

"T.J. is a charming little boy," the teacher was saying. "Very bright, and very well-mannered. The kind of child who's always been a pleasure to have in my classroom."

Olivia waited for the inevitable *but,* twisting the strap of her handbag in her fingers.

"But I've noticed that T.J. tends to be subdued around the other children. He hasn't seemed to make friends or even interact with the other children, and although that isn't necessarily a sign of any kind of serious problem, his reticence is a bit unusual at this age. Is there anything going on at home that might be weighing heavily on him?"

"No," Olivia said quickly.

Too quickly, she sensed from the level look the teacher gave her.

"I mean, he's acting fine at home," she said with more restraint. "He's not quiet or subdued. Sometimes I can't seem to shut him up," she added with a nervous chuckle, though that wasn't exactly the truth.

"I've noticed that he seems fairly comfortable around me and around my student teacher, on a one-on-one basis," Mrs. Starkey said. "But he does need to interact with his peers as well. Does he have any friends or siblings his own age?"

Friends?

Olivia thought of elderly Dr. Klimek.

She also thought of Max Rothwell's young twins, but shoved them out of her mind.

"Friends? Not really," she admitted. "No siblings, either."

"Young relatives, then? Perhaps cousins?"

"No," she said quickly, not wanting to get into any talk about extended family, or lack thereof. "There are no cousins."

"Well, in that case, I think it would be beneficial to T.J. for you and your husband to intervene in his social life as it were," the teacher said. "I would strongly suggest that you try to arrange some play dates with other children."

Olivia fumbled for a response. "I—I don't really know any of the children in his class, or their mothers."

"I understand. A good way to get to know them is to get involved. May I sign you up to be on the committee for our PTA's annual rummage sale? We're desperate for volunteers."

"I—" Olivia felt trapped once again. If she said no, it would seem as though she were standoffish and unwilling to do her part, let alone oblivious to her child's needs.

The teacher was probably thinking, *No wonder poor little T.J. is so antisocial—his mother doesn't want anything to do with anybody around here.*

"All right," she found herself blurting out. "I'll help."

"Wonderful." Mrs. Starkey smiled. "The sale isn't for a few weeks yet, but we will be having a meeting before then. In the meantime, perhaps I can explain your situation to one or two of the mothers of T.J.'s classmates so that they can include your son when their children play together after school—"

"No, you don't have to do that," Olivia interrupted. The last thing she wanted was for the other kids to feel as though T.J. were being forced upon them. She knew how kids could be. They'd make him miserable, teasing him that he couldn't make friends of his own.

Mrs. Starkey looked startled by her curt interruption.

"I can make other arrangements," Olivia said more mildly, but the teacher was looking at her as though she were a student trying to worm her way out of an assignment.

"You do understand that he needs the interaction with other children?"

"I do. I have two children in mind, in fact. Twins. Just T.J.'s age. I'll set up a play date with them."

She had no intention of doing so, of course. She didn't want to see Max Rothwell again.

Besides, T.J. would be fine. She could bring him out of his shell by spending more time with him, paying more attention to him. That was all he needed. Not play dates with children whose father was unnervingly handsome—and available.

"Good. I'll look forward to meeting with you next week to hear how things go. I think we should work together on this. I'll continue to try to draw T.J. out in the classroom. I've partnered him with the most popular child, Kenny Malone, for his geography project. That should help."

"Thank you," Olivia murmured.

"Don't worry, Mrs. Halloran. T.J. will soon be in the thick of things. Some children just need a nudge. Now, if you'll excuse me, I do have to run to my dentist appointment. I lost a filling last night and it's really beginning to bother me."

"Of course." Olivia rose and walked to the door as the teacher began pulling down the window blinds. "Thank you for your concern, Mrs. Starkey."

"That's my job. Don't worry, Mrs. Halloran. T.J. will be fine. I'll keep him under my wing until he's ready to fly on his own."

Olivia fought the impulse to roll her eyes at the bird

analogy. The teacher's voice had a slightly singsong quality and the precise diction of one who speaks regularly to small children. It was beginning to wear on her nerves.

As she walked back down the hall to the office, she thought again about her promise to set up a play date with the Rothwell twins.

This time, she felt a prickle of guilt. Maybe she should go through with it. For T.J.'s sake.

After all, the teacher must know what she was talking about. And Olivia wanted what was best for him.

She couldn't keep him locked away from the rest of the world forever, could she?

But you aren't. You're sending him to school—and that decision was hard enough to reach.

In fact, part of the reason she had decided to do so was that she figured it would call more attention to him if she kept him at home. People would think that was odd, and in a small town, anything odd soon became the topic of gossip.

Max Rothwell home-schooled his kids.

Why?

Did people gossip about him? If so, she wouldn't know. She never talked to anyone.

Clearly, the man was determined to maintain his privacy, and that of his children.

Which made them, in theory, the ideal companions for her and T.J.

Max could keep to himself; she could keep to herself, and their children could play together.

Maybe just once.

Just so T.J.'s teacher would realize that Olivia was cooperating with whatever was deemed necessary for his normal development.

But what if T.J. grew attached to Sam and Lindsey? What if he wanted to be friends with them? That would mean seeing Max on a regular basis, and she just couldn't do that.

Could she?

Not if she didn't want temptation, and a constant reminder that he was a virile, available man and she was a woman who had been lonely and celibate for far too long. The mere memory of Max in those tight jeans and that flannel shirt that strained over his muscular upper body . . .

Okay, Max Rothwell and his kids were out of the question.

She sighed as she opened the door to the office and saw T.J. sitting there, head bent over his crayons and paper.

He looked small and alone.

His face lit up when he raised his head and saw her.

"Mom!" he said. "Can we go now?"

"Sure."

She ruffled his hair, her heart swelling with love for him—and guilt that she'd put her own worries ahead of concern for him.

I'd do anything for you, kiddo, she told him silently. *Anything.*

FOUR

"Olivia."

"Hi," she said, and hesitated as though she were about to say his name, but wasn't sure what to call him.

"It's Max," he told her.

"I know," she said, and he felt like a jerk.

Of course she knew. She was here, wasn't she? Standing on his porch. With her son, who was clinging to her hand, wearing a shy-but-slightly-eager expression.

But then, she hadn't called him by his first name, or even his last, when she telephoned to set up the play date a few days ago. She had simply said in a rush when he answered the phone, "It's Olivia, from Doctor Klimek's office. I got your note. When do you want to get the kids together?"

Stunned that she had returned the call, much less agreed to the play date, he had said, "How about Saturday at noon?"

"Fine."

He had given her instructions to his place; she had thanked him, and that had been it.

Now, it was Saturday at noon, and he found himself tongue-tied, staring at her.

She wore faded jeans and an oatmeal-colored sweater beneath a hunter-green barn coat with a tan corduroy collar. Her hair was loose, and the chilly air had reddened her cheeks.

She was striking, but it was more than that. There was something in her eyes, something vulnerable and needy that made him want to reach out to her, made him want to say, *I'm here. You're not alone.*

But of course she was alone.

He wasn't *here,* not in the sense that his fantasies wanted him to be. He wasn't her protector or her lover or even her friend.

They were strangers, strangers whose children were going to play together. That was all.

The children needed each other. Not the parents.

He would do well to remember that.

Before he could snap out of his reverie and invite her in, there were pounding foot—and paw—steps behind him. Sam, Lindsey, and Lady appeared.

The twins quickly enveloped T.J. as Lady barked excitedly and pranced around them. The next thing Max knew, they had disappeared up to the loft to play a computer game and he and Olivia were left alone together.

He was still in the doorway—she, on the porch, looking as uncertain as he felt.

"Come in," he said finally, and stepped back.

She hesitated. "Maybe I should just leave him and come back. I didn't think he'd be so quick to warm up to the kids, but . . . I mean, it isn't as though he needs me to be here."

I need you, Max thought, despite himself.

"Stay," he said, hoping it didn't sound too fervent. "There's no need to drive all the way back to town and then turn around and come right back out here again to pick him up. Besides, I just made coffee. And I could use some adult conversation . . . know what I mean?"

She smiled.

It dazzled him, that smile, the way it lit her whole face, crinkling and twinkling her eyes.

It was the first time he had seen it, and it suited her.

There was something about her that didn't seem in sync with the reserved, skittish woman he had met that day in the vet's office. It was as though she were pretending to be someone she wasn't—as though there were another Olivia imprisoned inside of her.

She gave off a restless energy despite her quiet, reticent demeanor; it was as though she were sizzling inside and doing her best not to show it.

She intrigued him, and he realized he had to know more about her. He had to.

No, he couldn't befriend her or protect her or make love to her or feed any of the other urges her mere existence seemed to have aroused in him these past few weeks. But he could talk to her. Just . . . talk.

He led her to the kitchen, trying to see his home through her eyes.

Did she see the rustic appeal in the simple whitewashed walls and wood-beamed ceiling? Had she noticed the bright patchwork wall hanging Sarah had made and the corner built-in bookcase he had made from wood he'd split and smoothed himself? Did she think there were too many framed photos of the kids on the mantel? Too many toys spilling from the chest in the corner?

Julia would have looked around this place and declared it too small, too cluttered, too provincial.

Julia, who had been born and raised in Newberry Cove but thought she was destined to be a Fifth Avenue princess, had dreamed of mansions and fine antiques and servants.

How could he never have seen her for what she was? How could he never have realized that she thought he was her ticket out of town? What had he been doing while she was spinning all those plans for their future?

Lusting after her beautiful body, no doubt.

Later, when he had seemed to be disappointing Julia at every turn, he had found himself bewildered by her constant criticism.

Yes, he had said he would like to move away from Newberry Cove after college, but how could he leave his father when he needed him most?

Yes, he had said he wanted to wait to start a family, but he had meant a few years at most—not a few decades.

Yes, he had promised to hire someone to help her when she discovered she was pregnant with twins, but he had meant an occasional baby-sitter or cleaning service, not a full-time nanny and a maid.

Why hadn't he listened to what she was saying all along?

If he had listened, he wouldn't have been in for such a rude awakening.

But Julia was gone.

He had to stop dwelling on the past.

He had to stop thinking that every woman he met had a Julia lurking somewhere inside her.

Still, he couldn't deny that Olivia Halloran wasn't to be taken at face value. He suspected that there was far more to her than met the eye—and in his experience, that couldn't be a good thing.

He turned to look at her as they walked into the kitchen and saw that she was, indeed, glancing around with interest. But as her gaze moved from the potbellied stove and red rocker in one corner to the small round table with its blue-and-white checkered cloth in another, her expression was one of admiration.

"This is really homey," she said.

Her words caught him off guard.

Not just because she was paying him a compliment, but because she had zeroed in on the one thing he was trying to achieve with this cottage.

Homey.

He was determined to make it that way for his children, to create the kind of household that didn't cry out for a woman's touch even though there was no mother to cut flowers and bake cookies and do whatever it was that mothers did.

He had no idea, really, what those things might be, although he suspected Sarah's occasional presence was a good indication.

He had been raised in a house that sorely lacked homey touches once his mother was gone.

His father, for all his career success and jovial attitude, didn't know the first thing about raising a family or creating a home. The place had been run-down and shabby; Max's meals had come from cans and cereal boxes, and no one had ever ironed his clothes or told him to make his bed.

Max couldn't bear to raise Sam and Lindsey in that kind of place.

Julia had laughed when he'd spent months hand-making cradles for them out of wood he'd cut himself and when he had insisted on papering the nursery in pale yellow paper with a nursery rhyme pattern.

They had been living in town then, in a rented apartment that Julia had loathed. She had never even bothered to unpack their wedding gifts, telling Max she couldn't bear to see the Waterford crystal and Royal Dalton china in such a dingy place.

After she died, Max had taken the crystal and china, still in their boxes, and sold them to a consignment shop in town.

He had used some of that money on the potbellied

stove, and there had been enough left over to buy the gingham print curtains that hung in the kitchen windows and bright-red braided rugs that lay on the floor and the bright-blue pottery-style plates and mugs that filled the glass-fronted cupboards.

The kitchen was the first room in the house he'd finished. Then the loft, where the twins slept in matching beds of whitewashed pine beneath Sarah's handmade patchwork quilts. There were built-in shelves and cupboards for their toys and books, and he'd even set up a television and VCR there so that they could watch their favorite Disney movies.

Outside, in the yard, he had built a wooden play set with swings and monkey bars. Then he had built window boxes for all the windows and planted a flower garden and surrounded a section of the front yard with a white picket fence.

Now, though it was still a work in progress, the place was shaping up to be—yes, quite *homey*. And Olivia Halloran had noticed.

"Thank you," he said, trying not to glow with pride as she looked around.

She motioned at the paint cans stacked in the corner. "Are you doing some work on the place?"

He laughed. "Definitely. Trying to make the rest of it livable."

"Livable?" She looked around the kitchen again and motioned at the living room through the doorway. "It seems to be in great shape."

"You haven't been inside my bedroom."

The words seemed so harmless before they spilled out of his mouth. Then they just hung in the air between them, like an unspoken invitation.

He cleared his throat.

Her cheeks were pink.

"My bedroom," he added quickly, trying not to allow himself to imagine her there, in his bed, without her jeans and sweater and jacket, "is the last frontier. That and the bathroom, through that door, which I'm going to be re-tiling this weekend. Then I have to put in a new sink cabinet and paint all the trim. And install a fan because it gets too humid in there after I take a shower. I figure I'll get to my bedroom sometime in the next year. But it doesn't matter because, if you want to know the truth, nobody ever goes in there but me."

"Oh." Her cheeks were bright red now.

Oh, God. He'd just managed to reveal more to her about his nonexistent sex life than he had to anyone, even Andy.

Why, oh why, had he ever said that? Did she think he was crudely hinting around?

He hadn't been.

But still, she must know he was attracted to her.

And unless he was completely off the mark, she felt the same way.

So, did she think he was suggesting that the two of them retire to his room while the kids were playing upstairs?

Was she thinking, even now, as he was, about what that would be like? Was she imagining what it would feel like to lie in his bed, in his arms, against him. No distance between them, just warm, naked skin and roaming hands; total abandonment of everything proper.

He felt his body tighten with the urgent need to make that happen.

Why couldn't the phone ring or one of the kids call him or something, anything, to break the awkward silence that now filled the kitchen?

Don't leave, he bid her silently. *I know I sound like some kind of bumbling Romeo, but I'm not. All I want is for you to sit here with me and we'll talk. Just talk. Nothing more, no matter how hard it is to drag my mind from that particular topic.*

"I'll pour you some coffee," he said at last, moving to the pot on the counter.

She didn't run for the door.

She merely said, "Thank you," sounding relieved.

He filled two mugs, then put some of Sarah's butterscotch chocolate chip cookies on a plate and carried everything to the table.

"Do you want milk and sugar?" he asked her, sitting and motioning for her to do the same.

"No, thanks. I take it black."

"So do I. But I tend to make it pretty strong these days," he said, rubbing at his eyes that burned from another fairly sleepless night.

"It's okay."

He noticed that her own eyes were shadowed. Why was *she* losing sleep?

Again, he wondered where she had come from, what she was doing here. He wanted to come right out and ask her, but he sensed that doing that would be the one thing guaranteed to send her racing for the door.

So, he controlled his impulses, asking only, as he reached for a cookie, "You're not from here originally, are you?"

He knew the answer, of course.

Newberry Cove was too small a town for him to wonder about that. If she had lived here, he would have known her.

"No," she said, "I'm not."

Something in her tone made him look up from the plate of cookies. He saw that expression on her face again, the semi-terrified one she had worn in the office that day, when she had seemed to recognize Sam and Lindsey.

He saw her hand shake as she lifted the mug to her lips, so violently that a few drops of coffee sloshed over the rim.

Part of him wanted to change the subject, fast, to spare her the discomfort the personal question seemed to have caused her.

But another part of him was fascinated . . . and curious . . . and suspicious.

So, he found himself asking, in a conversational tone, as though it were the most casual inquiry in the world and he weren't waiting breathlessly for her answer, "Where *are* you from?"

She shrugged. "I don't really consider any one place home. I've moved around a lot."

"Oh, were you a military brat?" he asked.

She nodded.

He didn't miss the relief in her eyes, or the sense that she had gratefully seized upon his suggestion as a plausible explanation.

He wondered what would have happened if he hadn't offered her such an easy out. How would she have explained her lack of roots? Would she have told the truth, whatever that was? Or would she have come up with some other lie?

Maybe she isn't lying, he reminded himself. *Maybe she really was a military brat.*

But he knew with an unsettling certainty that it was a lie. She had something to hide, just as he had suspected the first time he met her.

Did Dr. Klimek know what it was? Was that why he had been so protective of her privacy?

"How long have you been in Newberry Cove?" he asked.

Another seemingly casual question, the kind of question you'd ask any newcomer in town.

So, why did her answer matter so much to him?

Why did he feel as though he were sticking his nose where it didn't belong?

And why did she look so panicky?

"A few years." she said. "Did you bake those cookies?"

"No, a friend did. Have one."

She seized a cookie the way she had seized his earlier suggestion—as though it were a way out of a dilemma.

He watched her bite into it, saw the way her hand trembled as she held it, and he wanted to reach out to steady her. He wanted to ask her what it was that had her so frightened; wanted to let her know that he wouldn't do anything to hurt her.

But they barely knew each other.

Despite the palpable attraction between them, he couldn't just come out with something so . . . well, so intimate.

So, to let them both off the hook, he told her about Sarah. About how she was always popping over with freshly baked cookies and cakes and how the twins had developed ferocious sweet tooths because of it. He described Sarah's mouth-watering double-fudge cake and the canoli she made from scratch and told her about the time he had decided to make them from the recipe he had copied from Sarah.

She actually smiled when he told her of his adventures trying to stuff the cheese filling into the pastry tubes, and she laughed out loud when he told her how in the end, when he had managed to make one perfect canoli, he had taken a bite—and found out he'd left out the sugar.

Thank God her hands were no longer trembling and she no longer looked as though she was about to bolt. He could hear the kids playing happily upstairs, and for a moment, he could almost convince himself that this could work—that their kids could be friends and that he and Olivia could have some kind of . . .

Not *relationship*.

To him, relationship meant romance, and there would be no more romance for him. Ever.

But maybe . . . maybe she could be someone for him to talk to. Sometimes.

Maybe he could rid himself of those pesky fantasies about her, and maybe they could see each other from time to time; compare notes on raising kids.

"So now that I've told you my adventures as a would-be Martha Stewart . . . do you bake?" he asked, fighting the most irrational impulse to brush away a sugary cookie crumb that was caught on her lip.

"Me? Sometimes. When I need a chocolate fix and we're out of Oreos."

Finally, she'd answered one of his questions without making him feel as though he'd invaded her life.

"Oh, yeah?" He took a sip of coffee, needing to take his eyes off that damn crumb. "What's your specialty?"

"Cream cheese brownies."

"With powdered sugar or chocolate frosting on top?"

"Are you kidding? Frosting. And not from a can."

There was something flirtatious about her now, as though she'd forgotten her problems, whatever they were. As though she'd let down her guard and let the real Olivia emerge—the Olivia he'd sensed was there all along.

She wasn't exactly lighthearted or animated as they discussed the merits of homemade frosting versus canned, but she had finally relaxed a bit.

That was why, when there was a lull in the conversation, he found himself saying, "You have a crumb on your lip."

It was an inane statement, really. The kind of thing he would say to one of the kids.

Just as what he did next was something he would do with one of the kids.

Just . . .

Reach out and brush the crumb away.

That was all he meant to do.

But when his thumb made contact with her soft, moist lower lip, he knew he had to taste it. He had to kiss her. He had to . . . or he would go out of his mind.

There was no time to stop and think, no time to check her expression and see how she had reacted to his brushing the crumb away.

He moved his hand from her lip to the back of her neck, tangling his fingers in her hair, and he pulled her face toward him. He leaned in and his mouth closed over hers.

Her lips were cookie-sweet and as silky soft as her hair, and they parted beneath his so easily that he was caught off guard.

It was as though she, too, had been anticipating this; as though she wanted it as much as he did.

He moaned deep in his throat as his mouth moved over hers, and he needed to be closer than this. Now that he had tasted her, he needed more. He needed . . .

She gasped.

Pulled away.

As though she had suddenly realized what was happening, and even before he looked into her eyes, he knew what he would find there.

It was back, of course. The panic and the fear that were so much a part of her that she seemed naked without them.

"Max," she said, her voice a whisper, her fingertips against her mouth as though she had been stung.

He couldn't speak. The sound of his name on her lips was shockingly intimate, and he realized this was the first time he had heard her say it.

He wanted to hear it again. He wanted to ask her to say it, but she was getting to her feet and she was moving quickly to the door.

He heard her call to T. J. before he could follow her into the living room.

"Olivia," he said, catching up to her as she stopped at the foot of the stairs leading up to the loft.

He touched her sleeve.

She spun on him. "Don't touch me," she said in a tone that was more distraught than angry.

He understood that he had violated some rule that had been written the moment they met.

Nothing would happen between them.

She wanted to be left alone.

Just as he had always wanted to be left alone after Julia. Always . . . until now.

He stood by as she went up to get T.J. and brought him down, protesting that he thought they were going to stay awhile longer. The twins and Lady were on their heels, Sam and Lindsey asking why T.J. had to leave and the dog barking as if to add her own complaint.

Before Max knew it, Olivia and T.J. were gone, having left without more than a cursory thank you from Olivia, who refused to meet Max's gaze.

"What happened, Daddy?"

"Why did T.J.'s mommy make him leave so fast?"

Because your Daddy kissed her senseless, that's why.

He merely shrugged, staring out at the empty driveway and the gray November rain.

FIVE

"Mrs. Halloran! We're so glad you could make it. Please, come in!"

Olivia hung back in the doorway of the school cafeteria for a moment, unable to move forward into the room. There were so many eyes upon her now that Mrs. Starkey had interrupted the meeting to address her.

She glanced over the two dozen or so faces, all belonging to mothers or fathers of children T.J.'s age. None were familiar. Of course not. She didn't know anybody in this town; she didn't want to know anybody.

Every one of these people was a potential threat. There was no telling if one of them might somehow recognize her despite her changed appearance. No telling whether someone might suddenly jump up and accuse her of being a kidnapper.

Then it would be all over.

The life she had so carefully constructed for herself and her son would be shattered. She would lose T.J. forever to the people who loathed her, people who would surely do everything in their power to turn him against her.

What are you doing here? This is insane, she told herself, feeling as though time had frozen as she stood in the doorway, poised on the threshold of self-destruction.

"Mrs. Halloran?" Mrs. Starkey prompted gently.
"There's a seat right over there . . ."

Olivia forced herself to move forward, to sink into the
half-sized chair the teacher had indicated at one of the
tables in the back. There were two other women sitting
there. She didn't dare look up at them, but she could
feel their curious gazes.

Why had she called so much attention to herself by
arriving late for this meeting?

She should have just gotten here on time so that she
could blend in with the rest of the crowd.

Instead, she had dawdled at Dr. Klimek's office, where
she had left T.J. in his care. She had watched as the two
of them worked to repair the wounded wing of a para-
keet, admiring the doctor's deft hands and her son's ability to follow his instructions.

The bond between T.J. and her boss was a strange one.
They seemed to talk about nothing but the animals, and
yet, neither seemed to need more than that. She had
eavesdropped on various conversations between them in
the past, noting how well Dr. Klimek's quiet observations
melded with T.J.'s little-boy eagerness.

When she had asked him to keep an eye on T.J. this
evening, the veterinarian had agreed readily, without asking where she had to go. She wondered if he suspected
that she was getting together with Max Rothwell. After
all, he knew about the note Max had left a few weeks
ago, and he must have overheard her when she called to
arrange that Saturday play date with him.

Tonight, she had made a point of telling Dr. Klimek
she was headed for the elementary school for a meeting.
He had nodded, and there was no telling whether he
believed her.

Now, as she heard Mrs. Starkey resuming the meeting

and felt some of the curious gazes shift away from her, she wished she were anywhere else. Even with Max.

No, not with Max, she hastily corrected. That was the last place she wanted to be.

After that kiss . . .

It had been on her mind ever since it had happened.

She found herself outraged at times, that he would do something so bold, so . . . well, so *wrong*.

But most of the time, she marveled that it hadn't felt wrong at all.

It had felt right to be sitting there with him in that cozy kitchen with the rain coming down outside and their children playing together upstairs—right for his mouth to be on hers, for his hand to be in her hair, for his tongue to slip past her lips . . .

She felt an uncomfortable tickle of heat ignite between her legs and was appalled that she had once again allowed her mind to wander to Max's kiss and what it had done to her.

With great effort, she shifted her attention to what Mrs. Starkey was saying.

But plans for a rummage sale weren't anywhere near as scintillating as thoughts of Max's kiss, and it wasn't long before her mind wandered right back to him.

She wondered if she were doomed to spend the rest of her life daydreaming about a man she barely knew.

Possibly.

After all, no man had kissed her like that since . . .

Well, no man had ever kissed her like that.

Of course, she hadn't been touched by a man since Thomas—nor would she be touched by a man again.

Not when this was what it did to her.

Left her with fantasies—not just about making love, but about other things, things that were just as forbidden.

She found herself picturing, at times, what it would be

like to live with him in that warm, inviting home he had created. She had imagined herself and T.J. enveloped in the kind of family life she had thought they would never have—siblings for T.J. and a dog and a daddy.

But that would mean marrying Max, and Max didn't want to get married.

Not only did Max not want to get married, she couldn't get married—not to anyone. It would mean trusting someone enough to tell him her secret, and she couldn't do that.

Because marriages didn't always last.

And if the day ever came when her new husband decided to hurt her, he could ruin her life by revealing her secret to the police.

So, she would remain alone, raising her son, wary of everyone who crossed her path.

She felt someone touch her arm and gasped, nearly bolting out of her seat.

"Oh, I'm so sorry! I didn't mean to make you jump."

She realized it had been the woman seated next to her and that the meeting seemed to have dissipated into a series of clustered conversations among the tables.

"I'm Lisa," the woman said. She was blond and pretty in an outdoorsy kind of way. "And this is Amy."

She indicated the third woman at their table. She was very overweight, her round face smiling at Olivia, framed by a cloud of dark, curly hair.

"You're T.J.'s mother," Amy said. "He's in Brian's class."

"I'm Olivia," she said, having never heard of Brian. She wished she had paid more attention to the list of classmates T.J. had brought home not long ago.

But her son had simply dumped it on the counter and she had glanced at it, then tossed it away. She wouldn't need it for birthday invitations; T.J. wouldn't be having a party or attending any of theirs if he got invited.

She couldn't tell Amy, "T.J. is always talking about Brian."

Nor did Amy say, "I've heard so much about T.J."

What she said was "T.J. is a wonderful little artist."

"He is?" Olivia asked, surprised. It was true, but how did Amy know?

"I volunteer in the classroom once a week," Amy said, as though she'd read her mind. "He's such a nice, quiet little boy."

Olivia smiled.

"My daughters are older—Ashley is in third grade with Brian's sister Jennifer, and Suzanne is in fifth," Lisa said, as if to explain why she didn't know anything about T.J. "You haven't lived in town very long, have you, Olivia?"

Her guard went up. "Not long, no."

"I didn't think so. How did you happen to move here?"

"I just . . . I thought it would be a nice place to raise T.J."

"It is a great town for families. Are you married?" Amy asked casually.

Olivia struggled to sound just as casual. "No . . . not anymore."

"Divorced? So am I, as of last month," Lisa said.

"Widowed."

"Oh." Lisa looked taken aback. "I'm so sorry."

"That's terrible," Amy put in.

Olivia shrugged and looked around. Was the meeting over? Could she escape?

"Well, I suppose we should figure out when we're going to get together and unpack the contributions to the rummage sale," Lisa said. "Since that's our appointed duty."

"I'm glad to be working behind the scenes this year," Amy said. "Remember last year, how crazy it was actually working the sale?"

"Was it ever. People were fighting over items," Lisa told

Olivia, who made an effort to look suitably amazed when all she could think about was that she had to get out of here.

"So this year, we volunteered to collect the donations in my garage," Amy said, "and unpack and organize them."

"Since you're sitting at our table, you can help us," Lisa told Olivia. "Unless you'd rather referee the customers at the sale . . ."

"No, thanks," Olivia said quickly, thinking that the last thing she wanted to do was be around a crowd. "I'll help you with the unpacking and organizing."

"Great. When are you free? Do you work?"

"She's Dr. Klimek's technician," Amy said. "Right?"

Startled, Olivia only nodded.

"I've seen you there when we bring my kids' cat Goober in for shots."

"I . . . I thought you looked familiar," Olivia lied. She tried to be careful to avoid seeing a lot of people while she was working. Mostly, she stayed in the back, with the animals.

"What hours do you work?"

"I can be flexible," Olivia said, which was the truth, for a change. "When do you need me to help you?"

"How about next Wednesday afternoon? By then we should have most of the contributions in. The best part about unpacking and organizing is that if we see anything we really want, we can grab it before it goes on sale," Amy confided.

Olivia forced an interested expression. "That sounds great."

"Yeah, you'd be surprised at what people give away. A few years ago I got a brand new Krups coffeemaker, still in the box," Lisa said.

Their conversation turned to a discussion of the various items they had found at past rummage sales.

Olivia murmured appropriate responses, but her thoughts wandered.

Naturally, she found herself thinking about Max again.

She hadn't seen or talked to him since she had fled that Saturday afternoon after he'd kissed her.

She didn't expect to have any further contact with him.

True, T.J. kept asking about Sam and Lindsey, wanting to know when they could come over and play with him.

She had put him off until now, which hadn't been too hard since he'd been in bed with a nasty cold for a week.

But she couldn't stall indefinitely.

Sooner or later, T.J. would figure out that his mommy had no intention of letting him see his new friends ever again.

It's so unfair to him, Olivia told herself with a pang of guilt.

But there was no way around it.

She couldn't expose herself again to Max Rothwell—and further temptation. There was only one place that could lead . . .

Into his arms.

That was still—and always would be—totally out of the question.

Max awoke the following Saturday morning to silence and the late autumn sun streaming through his bedroom window.

Sun?

That meant it was morning . . .

Silence?

Instinctively he knew something was wrong.

If the sun was up, so were the kids. And they were never quiet.

He bolted out of bed, stepping over a toolbox but stub-

bing his toe on a box of fixtures he'd removed from the
bathroom wall during the tiling job.

"Damn," he said, hopping on one foot and rubbing
his toe. "Sam? Lindsey?" he called, making his way to
the bedroom door and peering out into the living room.

There was no reply.

His gut twisted.

"Sam? Lindsey?"

Panic edged into his voice as he raced up to the loft,
finding their beds empty—and neatly made.

Something was very wrong.

The kids never made their beds until he told them to.

Where the hell were they?

And where was Lady?

His gaze fell on a sheet of paper taped to the lamp on
the bedside table. It took him a moment to decipher the
crayoned letters.

Daddy,
Don't wurry. Well be hom tonit.
Sam and Lindsey

"Christ," he said aloud, his heart pounding.

He headed back downstairs to call Andy and throw on
his clothes.

Olivia was putting clean laundry into a drawer in T.J.'s
dresser when she heard the knock on the front door.

She froze.

"Hey, Mom, the door! I'll get it!" T.J. yelled.

"No, T.J., wait. I'll get it," she called, and rushed toward the front of the house.

Of course her son was excited and intrigued.

Nobody ever knocked on their door—except whenever
the meter reader came from the local gas company and
when the mailman had stopped one time to tell her that

a tree branch had fallen on top of her box in a storm, crushing it.

But the meter had been read a few weeks ago, and today, there was no storm. The sun shone brightly outside the windows.

Now, as she approached the front door, Olivia felt her heart pounding. Was it the police? Or . . .

Worse?

He's found me, she thought, seized by dread. *He's here, and he's going to take T.J. away.*

There was another knock.

Standing a few feet back, she looked through the windowed part of the door but saw no one.

She bit her lip and clenched her trembling hands.

T.J., behind her, asked, "Aren't you going to open it, Mom?"

"There's no one there."

As if to disprove her, another knock promptly sounded. Perplexed, Olivia took another step toward the door.

That was when she saw them . . .

The tops of two small blond heads.

She knew who was there, then, and her heart sank.

It wasn't the police, and it wasn't the man she had come to dread . . .

No, Sam and Lindsey were here.

And that had to mean their father was, too.

Bracing herself for a confrontation with the man who had haunted her thoughts for weeks now, she took a deep breath and opened the door.

"Hey!" T.J. said behind her and squealed with delight as he saw who it was. "What are you guys doing here?"

"We came to play," Sam said solemnly.

"Can we come in? I have to use the bathroom," Lindsey said urgently, her legs crossed.

Between them, Lady barked.

"Where's your dad?" Olivia asked, confused. There didn't seem to be any sign of Max. Just two bikes parked at the foot of the steps.

"He's home."

She didn't miss the guilty expression in Sam's eyes before he looked down at his sneakers.

"How on earth did you get here? And how did you know where we lived?"

"T.J. told us," Lindsey said, bouncing on her crossed legs.

"You didn't ride your bikes all the way here?"

"It wasn't that far."

A few miles, at least, Olivia thought incredulously.

"Can I use the bathroom, Olivia?" Lindsey asked again. "Please? It's an emergency."

"Sure, honey. It's right through there," she said, pointing the way.

The little girl scurried away down the hall.

"Come on, Sam, let's go play in my room," T.J. said. "Mom, tell Lindsey where we are when she comes out."

"Not so fast," Olivia cut in, with a hand on T.J.'s shoulder. "Your dad is probably worried sick about you two, Sam."

"Nah. I left him a note 'cause he was sleeping when we left."

"A note?" She thought of Max waking up to find his kids missing. "Sam, we've got to get you back home."

"No! We want to play with T.J. . . . please, just for a little while. We never get to go anywhere or have any fun."

"But you can't just leave home without your dad's permission. Look at what happened to the two of you the last time you pulled this. You would have drowned . . ." She shuddered at the memory.

"But you saved us," Sam said matter-of-factly. "Thanks

so much, Olivia. That was great of you. Can't we just go
play in T.J.'s room now?"

"Nope. Your dad must be going crazy."

"I told you, we left a—"

"What if he didn't see it?"

"Well, can't you just call my dad and tell him where
we are, then?"

"I can't," she said. "Even if I wanted to. We don't have
a phone."

"No phone?" Sam frowned.

She saw T.J. looking at Sam, dismayed, as though realizing that his friend thought it was odd that there was no
phone in their home.

He's worried, she realized, *that he's going to lose Sam's
friendship. And I'm doing nothing to ease his fears. Instead I'm
doing everything I can to keep him away from the Rothwells.*

Olivia reached out and put one hand on T.J.'s shoulder
and one on Sam's. "Listen, boys," she said, "we can't let
Sam and Lindsey's daddy worry. That wouldn't be right,
would it?"

"I guess not," Sam said.

"So, we're going to have to go find him and tell him
you're all right. But maybe your daddy and I can talk,
and if he agrees, we'll set up another play date for all of
you."

"Today?"

"I don't know if your dad is going to want you to have
any special privileges today after what you did, but that's
up to him," Olivia said.

Lindsey came out of the bathroom, trailing her denim
overall straps. "Olivia, can you help me with these?" she
asked shyly.

"Sure." Olivia crouched beside her and buttoned the
straps into place. She fought the urge to fix the strands
of hair escaping from Lindsey's messy braids.

She wasn't the little girl's mother, after all.

But Lindsey doesn't have a mother of her own.

She found herself wondering, not for the first time, about the mother the twins had lost—the wife Max had lost.

Was she the reason Max didn't want to remarry? Had he loved her so much that he couldn't bear to let another woman replace her?

Of course that was it.

She found herself envying him, wishing she knew what it was like to mourn a dead spouse instead of hating him with all her soul—and feeling guilty because of it.

"Come on," she said, straightening and addressing all the kids. "I'll drive you home."

"What about Lady and our bikes?"

"Lady can come. But the bikes . . . your dad will have to come get them another time, in his truck."

Which meant she wouldn't be seeing the last of Max Rothwell today.

She found herself trying to ignore a glimmer of pleasure at the thought.

Max was pacing the living room when he saw Olivia's car turn into the driveway. He somehow knew, even before he spotted their two heads in the back seat, that Sam and Lindsey were with her. Lady, too.

Relief shot through him as he ran to the door, flung it open, and raced outside. He met the car at the end of the driveway, opening the back door and freeing the kids from their seatbelts to scoop them into his arms.

"Thank God," he said raggedly against their blond hair. "Thank God, you're safe."

Only when his overwhelming joy had subsided did he think to scold them.

"How could you just take off like that? Where did you go? What's the matter with you? After what happened last time—"

"But, Daddy, Olivia rescued us again," Sam said.

"She's our guardian angel, remember?" Lindsey added hopefully.

For the first time, he allowed his attention to shift to Olivia, sitting behind the wheel in the front seat, T.J. strapped in beside her.

"Thanks for bringing them home," he said, his voice still hoarse with emotion. "Where did you find them?"

"At my front door. They came to visit T.J."

"Oh, Lord . . ." He shook his head. "You went all that way? But how—"

"On their bikes," Olivia informed him. "We left them at my house."

"How did they know where you lived?"

"T.J. told us when he was here that day," Sam said.

"Don't be mad, Daddy. Olivia said we can all be friends if you say it's okay."

"Olivia said that?" He looked over at her. He couldn't read the expression in her eyes.

"She said we could play together, maybe even today."

"I said I didn't think your daddy would want you to do it today after what happened, but that's up to him," she interjected quickly.

"Olivia is right. I don't think you should have any special privileges today."

"That's exactly what Olivia said. *Special privileges,*" Sam said.

"Did she?" He flashed her a look.

He hated himself for wanting her in that moment. How could he be thinking of something like that at a time like this? His children had been missing; he'd spent the last hour pacing the floor and waiting for the phone to ring,

knowing Andy and the other cops were combing the town
for Sam and Lindsey . . .

But they're here now, he reminded himself. *Safe and sound.*

*They would never have left on their own in the first place if
you hadn't screwed things up with T.J.'s mother so that they
can't play together anymore.*

"Listen, why don't you come in," he said to Olivia as
he released the kids and they clambered out of the car,
followed by Lady. "Not for an official play date, but
just . . . I need to sort things out. I have to call Andy
down at the police station and let him know I've found
the kids. He might want to talk to you."

The moment he mentioned the word *police,* her eyes
widened.

He wasn't mistaken about her reaction. He saw her
hands tighten on the steering wheel.

"Oh, I don't think that'll be necessary. I told you, they
came over to play with T.J., so I drove them home. Ask
them. They'll tell you."

He glanced at T.J. and saw that he was talking to Sam
and Lindsey through his open window, not listening to
the conversation. "Of course I believe that's what happened, Olivia," Max said to her in a low voice. "Why
wouldn't I? You think I doubt your word?"

"Of course not! Why would you—"

"I wouldn't. That's what I'm saying."

His thoughts were spinning.

Was she in some kind of trouble? Was that why she
didn't want to talk to the police?

Or was she just reluctant to come in because it would
mean being alone with him again?

There was no way of knowing.

He took a deep breath. "I just—Okay, Olivia, I'll admit
that the real reason I want you to come in isn't because
I think the police will want to talk to you about this. Andy

is my friend. He'll just be glad I found the kids. The reason I want you to come in . . ."

He paused.

She was looking straight ahead, out the windshield, her hands still clenched on the wheel.

"I wanted to see you again. After what happened the other day. Not so that it can happen again," he added hastily. "I just want to prove to you that it won't. That we can have a civilized, platonic relationship. For the kids' sake."

She swallowed audibly but said nothing.

"Look, it wouldn't be fair to keep the kids apart. Mine are lonely. So is T.J. They all like each other. What harm can it do to let them be friends?"

What harm can it do? he echoed his own words incredulously.

It can do a lot of harm.

What if you fall in love with her?

Not only did you swear you'd never fall for another woman again, but this one obviously has baggage. You know she's hiding something, just as Julia was.

But what Julia had been hiding was the selfish, shallow, nasty side that would ultimately ruin their marriage and take her own life.

Olivia might not be showing him her true self, but she couldn't possibly be capable of the cold-hearted acts Julia had pulled on him.

No, Olivia was a good person. That much, he knew instinctively.

But she was hiding something, and whatever it was, he couldn't get involved.

Not emotionally.

Not romantically.

Yet how could he see her on a regular basis, because

of the kids, without letting his attraction surface once again? It burned hotly every time he saw the woman.

You'll just have to learn to quell it, he told himself. *You can't let it take over the way it did when you kissed her the other day. You'll have to learn self-control.*

And there was no time like the present to start.

"Come in, Olivia," he said again. "For T.J.'s sake. Okay?"

He must have struck the magic chord when he uttered her son's name. He saw her glance at the boy, then at Sam and Lindsey out the window.

Then, finally, her eyes settled on him.

"Okay," she said softly. "I'll come in, but just for a little while."

"Good." He successfully overcame the urge to break into a huge grin or start dancing with joy.

See? he told himself, pleased. *Self-control. Nothing to it.*

SIX

"Okay, they're watching a video up there. *Beauty and the Beast.* Is that okay?"

Olivia spun around at the sound of Max's voice behind her as he descended the steps from the loft.

"It's . . . fine. *Beauty and the Beast?* That's fine."

Carefully, she averted her gaze from the photo on the mantel, the one she'd been staring at.

It sat amidst clusters of other photos, most of them showing the twins at various ages and holidays, and all of them snapshots.

This one, however, was a professional, posed portrait in a silver frame. It showed a woman, an elegantly beautiful woman who could only be the children's mother. Her coloring was dark while theirs was fair; but, looking at her face, Olivia recognized their delicate features and porcelain coloring.

She was as beautiful as Max was. They must have been a striking couple.

"That's Julia," Max said flatly, and she realized he had caught her looking.

"Your wife?"

He seemed to hesitate, his thumbs looped in the pockets of his faded Levis as he contemplated her question.

Then he nodded. "But she's not—I mean, she died not long after the twins were born."

"I know. How?" As soon as the question had left her lips, she wished she could take it back. It was too personal, too painful a question to ask a man she barely knew.

But he didn't look upset. He answered in a matter-of-fact tone. "She was killed in a car accident with a tractor trailer. On Christmas Eve," he added.

"Oh, my God. That's so awful, Max," she said, clasping a hand to her lips.

She glanced again at the woman in the photo. What a tragic waste. She should be here, in this home, raising her children. Loving her husband.

"It was awful," he agreed.

She turned. "Were you . . . were you with her? When it happened?"

Now a pained expression did cross his face, and she instantly regretted asking yet another prying question.

"No, I wasn't with her," he said, so tersely that she knew he was irritated with her for dragging this up.

"I'm sorry—" she began.

"She was with someone else," Max said. "He was killed, too."

Stunned at the implication, Olivia didn't know what to say.

"It's okay," Max told her, "I'm used to it by now. In fact, I knew even then what was going on. He had money. He was going to leave his wife and kids for her, and the two of them were going to start over again in New York. That's where Julia always wanted to be."

"I'm so sorry, Max," she said sincerely, realizing she'd been so wrong about him still being in love with his dead wife. There was no mistaking the anger in his voice.

"It's all right. It was a long time ago. But the kids . . . they don't know. About Julia."

"About how she died?"

"They know there was an accident and that it was on Christmas. That's why Lindsey is so interested in angels. She thinks her mother is one." He gave a brittle laugh. "I hope she never finds out how wrong she is."

"It's good that you didn't tell the children the truth about her," Olivia said.

He looked up at her. "You say that as if you know from experience. Is there a nasty ex-husband in your past, Olivia?"

"He's dead, too," she said hesitantly.

"I'm sorry. Were you happy with him?"

The question was stark, personal . . . as personal as what she'd just asked him. And he had answered.

She owed him the same candor, if not the whole truth.

"No, we weren't happy," she told Max. "Not by the time he died. But I never told T.J. . . . ."

"What a miserable human being his daddy was?"

She nodded, thinking, *that, and a whole lot of other details.*

"What else is there, Olivia?" Max asked.

"What do you mean?" Confused, she stared at him.

"What other painful things from your past are haunting you still?"

Stunned at his question, she found herself taking a step away from him, as though the closer he got, the easier it would be for him to read her thoughts.

"I . . . nothing is haunting me," she told him nervously. "I just don't like to talk about it, that's all. You must know how it is. You just want to put a bad marriage and a death behind you."

"I do know how that is," he said, nodding. "I'm sorry. I didn't mean to poke my nose where it doesn't belong. But I can't seem to help it where you're concerned. Listen, I'm going to go call Andy and tell him the kids are back. Have a seat. I'll build a fire when I get off the phone."

"A fire? But it's not . . ."

But he had already left the room.

Actually, it was chilly in here. A fire would be nice.

The sun was no longer shining outside, she noticed, glancing at the bay window above the couch. The sky was overcast, the clouds tinged with more charcoal black than milky gray. That meant snow.

She hadn't heard the weather forecast in a few days, but she wouldn't be surprised if there were a chance of flurries.

She heard Max in the next room, talking on the phone to his police officer friend. She held her breath, eavesdropping, praying the cop wouldn't want to question her.

"No, she's just their friend's mother," she heard Max saying. "She drove them home . . . Yeah, she is . . . Come on, Andy, the kids are right upstairs . . . Very funny. Listen, I have to go . . . right. Thanks a lot for the search. I swear it won't happen again. They're going to be locked up until they're twenty-one. 'Bye."

Moments later, he came back into the room, carrying an armload of wood. He busied himself by the fireplace, and soon there was a blazing fire on the hearth.

"That's better," he said, glancing at her. "This place is so drafty that it feels cold no matter how high I turn the thermostat. On winter nights the kids and I often sleep right here in front of the fireplace in sleeping bags."

"That sounds like fun," she said, so struck by the cozy image of an indoor camp-out that she was numb with jealousy.

They were so much like a real family, the three Roth-wells, even though a woman's presence was so conspicuously missing. In contrast, her lonely life with T.J. seemed almost pathetic. Yet what could she do about it?

T.J. would never have a daddy or a sibling.

T.J. would have only her—that was why she had to be everything to him. The perfect mother.

And she was failing him miserably.

As if to punctuate her dismal thought, a squeal of laughter came from the loft above.

T.J.'s voice.

He was happy here, with Max's kids.

Why?

Because T.J. had let them in the way he had let Dr. Klimek in, she realized. Until now, her son had followed her example, trusting no one but the old veterinarian. That was why he hadn't made friends in school, why he kept to himself. That was all he knew how to do.

Then Sam and Lindsey had come along. They were so open, so loving, so hungry for a friend their own age— they had reached out to him the way no other children had, and he had been receptive.

"The kids are having fun up there," Max said, as though he'd read her thoughts again.

"They are."

"Makes me think that maybe it was wrong of me to home-school them."

"Why are you, then?"

He sat next to her on the couch. Not close enough to make her uncomfortable, but close enough that she could feel the heat of his body and smell the wood smoke clinging to his clothing.

How she would love to snuggle up next to him here in front of the fire. The very idea was so inviting that she forgot she had asked him a question until he began answering it.

"I didn't want to be a part of Newberry Cove anymore," he said thoughtfully. "Not in any way. That's why I moved out here after Julia died. You know, I used to be the mayor."

"I know."

When he looked surprised, she said, "I read it in the paper."

"Oh, yes. Right. In that article about the mysterious angel who had rescued Sam and Lindsey from the water. I never really thanked you, you know."

"It's okay."

"No, it isn't. You saved my kids. There's nothing more precious to me in this world than those two little people, Olivia. Nothing."

"I know how you feel," she said, struck by the fierce parental love etched in his voice, on his face.

They had been through similar experiences, she reminded herself. Now they were both, in their own way, trying to make up for what their lost spouses couldn't give to their children—couldn't have given even if they had lived.

That was why Max was so protective of his twins, so determined to keep them safely under his wing.

And it was, in part, why Olivia was the same way about T.J.

With one difference.

But Max couldn't know about that. She had to fight the temptation to trust him, to open up to him about anything else. He couldn't know. It was too risky.

"Why aren't you the mayor of Newberry Cove anymore?" she asked abruptly to change the subject. "And—forgive me for saying it, but you don't exactly look like a politician."

"I don't?" He flashed a brief grin. "You're kidding."

She smiled back and indicated his shaggy hair, his

jeans. "I know this is a small town, but you look more like the lumberjack type."

"Good. The first thing I did when I resigned was grow my hair and dump all my suits and ties and dress shirts into the Goodwill bin."

"Why did you resign?" she asked again.

The remnants of his grin promptly vanished. "Because I didn't want all the attention that focused on me and my kids. After Julia was killed—people talked. It seemed I was the last one to have found out what was going on with her. The infidelity, I mean. I felt betrayed, Olivia. Not just by Julia. By them. I had spent my whole life feeling that I owed them something . . ."

"Owed whom?"

"The people of Newberry Cove."

"But why?"

He gave a short, bitter laugh. "I forgot. You're not from here. You don't know about my father."

"Tell me." She rested her chin on her hand, watching him in the flickering firelight as a faraway look drifted over his features.

"He was a born politician," Max said. "If Jack Rothwell hadn't been committed to small-town life, he would have been president. As it was, he was mayor of Newberry Cove for as long as I can remember. My mother used to tease him that he sometimes acted as though he were married to the town. After she died, he threw himself into politics more than ever."

"When did she die?"

"I was just a kid. It happened when she gave birth to my sister."

"You have a sister?" For some reason, the news shocked her. Everything about Max Rothwell pegged him as a loner. When he had mentioned Andy's mother Sarah the

other day, she had gotten the impression that the kindly
older woman was the closest thing to family in Max's life.

"Yeah. Tessa," Max said, grief so clearly carved in his
eyes that Olivia knew he had lost her. "My father was so
shattered after losing my mother that I pretty much raised
her."

"But you were just a kid yourself."

He nodded. "I was nine years older. Old enough to
take care of her while my father was busy with his own
life, running the town. He always said that the people of
Newberry Cove were our family. That we should be grateful everyone cared so much about us. People used to
bring over food for us sometimes—the poor motherless
family. But most of the time, Tessa and I fended for our-
selves because Dad couldn't be there."

Olivia shook her head, marveling at all he had been
through.

"Anyway," he said, "I met Julia when I was in high
school. She was a few years younger. Tessa couldn't stand
her, of course. I just thought she was jealous of the time
I gave to Julia. Now I know that no one in their right
mind would be as crazy about Julia as I was. But I didn't
see her for what she really was. Not then. I graduated
from high school and went off to college in Boston, but
I came home as often as I could to see Julia and take
care of Tessa. That was when my sister started to run
wild . . . when I wasn't around all the time to keep tabs
on her."

"It wasn't your responsibility, though."

"Yes, it was. By that time, my father's health was failing.
He had a heart condition. The stress of overworking himself didn't help. He was a small-town mayor, but he
treated the job as though he were governor, or president.
He was always talking about not letting anyone down. He

meant the people of Newberry Cove. He never realized he'd let both me and Tessa down."

"That's so sad."

"It gets worse." Max sighed. "Julia graduated and came to school in Boston. I found a job and started working on my master's degree."

"In what?"

"Education. I wanted to be a teacher. Julia didn't approve. She thought I should major in business. She wanted me to become some kind of tycoon. She thought we were going to get married and move to New York. Actually, I didn't argue with her. Don't ask me why. I guess I just figured that she had big dreams, but in the end she would be content to go back to Newberry Cove and settle down, the way I wanted to. I had to, really. I couldn't leave Tessa behind."

"What happened?" Olivia asked, so caught up in his story that for the first time since she'd met him, she forgot about her own situation, and the fact that she was supposed to keep a safe emotional and physical distance from this man.

"I moved home to write my thesis and keep an eye on Tessa. I knew she had fallen in with a bad crowd. Julia was finishing her senior year in Boston and planning our wedding when Tessa died."

"She died? Oh, God, Max, I'm so sorry. What happened to her?"

"Drugs."

Even now, after all these years, there were tears glistening in his eyes.

Olivia reached out and touched his sleeve, forgetting that she shouldn't go near him.

He didn't flinch or pull away or acknowledge it in any way. He seemed lost in his own tragic past.

She left her hand there, needing to comfort him more

than she needed to stay away from him. At least, for right now.

"It pretty much killed my father, losing her. He realized, I think, then, that he hadn't been there for Tessa. He blamed himself for her death. He dropped dead a few months after she died."

"Oh, Max. I'm so sorry."

"I had married Julia by then. We were saving money to move to New York. But when my father died, I caved in to the pressure to take over the remainder of his term in office." His tone was laced with bitterness when he added, "After all, I owed the town. They were my family. Hadn't I heard that my whole life?"

"So you followed in his footsteps."

"Exactly. And the strange thing is, I found that I liked it. I liked being busy. I liked working with people, helping them, solving problems, feeling as though I were accomplishing something. Julia couldn't understand it."

"Why not?"

He smirked. "She didn't see how I thought that I could be happy staying here in Newberry Cove. But I had these visions of doing it right—doing what my father couldn't do. Maybe I had something to prove to everyone—to him."

He sighed, staring into the fire and shifting his weight on the couch.

Olivia grew conscious of his muscle tensing beneath his flannel sleeve as he moved. She pulled her hand away, not wanting a reminder that beneath the flannel was his bare, strong arm. She didn't want to wonder what he looked like, shirtless, with those biceps and those broad shoulders . . .

"I wanted children," he was saying, softly. "I wanted them so badly. I needed to take care of someone the way

I had taken care of Tessa—no, the way I would have if I had done it right."

"You were just a kid yourself, Max."

"I know. But if I hadn't gone away to school, she would be here."

"You can't know that."

He shrugged. "Julia didn't want a family until we moved to New York and started what she called our 'real' life. But she got pregnant accidentally. She didn't want to continue the pregnancy. I convinced her that the timing was right. Then, when we found out it was going to be twins, she was distraught. By then it was too late for her to terminate—"

"Do you think she would have?"

"I found out later she had tried. The doctor wouldn't perform the procedure at that stage. But I never knew that. And I promised her it would be great. She was miserable throughout the pregnancy. Really sick. Complaining about the weight gain. And as soon as the kids were born, she started running around while I watched the kids. She made it seem that I owed her because she had given up nine months of her life already. She made up for that pretty quickly."

"Was that when she started having an affair?" Olivia asked, resenting the woman who had so callously hurt him and their children.

"*Affairs.* I'm pretty sure there was more than one. By that time, I knew she wouldn't stick around, and I didn't want her to. I didn't want the kids getting hurt by her any more than they would be when they realized she'd never be a real mother to them. Then she died. And the gossip went full speed ahead. That's why I got out of town."

"You didn't go far."

"No. Where could I go? This area is the only home

I've ever known. Much as I wanted to pull up all the stakes and move across the country, start over—I just couldn't do that for some reason."

His words hit close to home for Olivia.

Pull up all the stakes . . . move across the country . . . start over . . .

Little did he know how difficult it really was.

Or maybe he did know. After all, he hadn't done it.

"Besides," he was saying, "I figured what money I had from Julia's and my father's life insurance policies and from selling my father's house would go further around here than someplace where the cost of living is higher— which is just about anyplace else. And I figured if I could keep the kids away from the gossip mill for a few years, until it settled down, then they would be protected from the truth about their mother. The trouble is, I don't think they'll ever be safe from the truth. At some point, some-body is going to tell them what really happened with Julia. I'd just as soon have it be me, but I'm not ready to do that. Not just yet."

"I don't blame you. They're still young."

"You haven't told T.J. about his father?"

His words startled her. For a moment, she had forgot-ten that she had told him anything at all about Thomas.

He doesn't know, she reassured herself, feeling jittery again. *Not the whole truth.* But still, why had she let any-thing slip? Anything at all? How could she have been so careless?

"No, T.J. doesn't know that his father and I weren't happily married," she said, trying to think of a way to change the subject again.

"Are you going to tell him?"

"Not unless I have to."

Damn, she thought as soon as the reply left her mouth. Why had she phrased it like that?

She looked at him, unable to read his expression. Was he suspicious?

"Why would you have to?" he asked, and his words seemed measured. "After all, you're not from here. Nobody knows you. Nobody knew your husband. You can keep it a secret his whole life if you want."

She nodded uncomfortably.

"I'm sorry he hurt you, Olivia," Max said unexpectedly.

His kind words settled into some needy place deep inside her, warming her despite her intention to keep him at bay.

"Is that why you haven't remarried?" he asked. "Because of the way he treated you?"

She could only nod again.

Don't give him anything else—not another shred of the truth. Don't start talking.

If you do, before you know it, you'll be spilling the whole sordid story, and you'll regret that.

If that happens, you'll have to leave.

Not just leave his house . . .

Leave Newberry Cove.

She wasn't willing to do that, she thought wearily. Not now, when T.J. was finally starting to seem like a normal kid.

Not now, when she had met Max.

No!

Max was the very reason she was thinking of leaving town.

He wasn't a reason to stay.

"What's the matter, Olivia?"

"What do you mean?"

"You just flinched, as if something bit you."

"Did I?"

"Are you all right? I mean, is there anything you want to talk to me about? I'm a good listener. And I owe you, after I spilled my whole sad story. You must have been bored out of your mind. Thanks for letting me get things off my chest."

"I wasn't bored," she said honestly. "I'm glad you told me."

If only she could unload her own burden.

Five years of silence had built up a terrible tension inside her, she realized.

She had never told her secret to a single soul. Never spoken aloud about it.

That was part of the reason, she supposed, that she had taken up jogging. It helped to work up a sweat, to exercise to the point of exhaustion so that she felt as if she'd drained herself of everything toxic—even if only for a short while.

I need a friend as much as T.J. does, she thought incredulously as utter loneliness infused her. *I need someone to talk to, someone who isn't six years old and utterly dependent on me.*

"It's snowing!"

The shout from the loft interrupted her thoughts, and she welcomed the distraction.

She looked out the window and saw that it was, indeed, snowing. Fat, fluffy white flakes swirled in the air. Already the tree branches were dusted in white.

"Can we go out and build a snowman?" Sam asked, bubbling over with excitement as the three children came pounding down the stairs.

"Or a snow woman?" Lindsey suggested significantly.

"A budding feminist," Max said dryly to Olivia. "Do you mind if they play outside?"

"If we go, too. I really don't like T.J. to be unsupervised."

"That's fine," he said hastily. "We can go for a walk in the woods. I like to walk in the snow at this time of year.

It's still a welcome sight. By February, I'm cursing the stuff, and by April . . ."

"Or May." She laughed. "I know what you mean."

"Okay, come on, everyone," Max said, getting up. "Sam, find your spare pair of boots for T.J. to borrow. They should fit."

The kids took off for the mud room off the kitchen, laughing and shouting excitedly.

Max looked at Olivia. "You're going to freeze."

She had on jeans and a long-sleeved white tee-shirt, and had worn her jean jacket over.

"Let me give you something else to wear," he said, and disappeared into the bedroom.

Moments later, as she mulled the decidedly intimate idea of wearing Max's clothes, he reappeared clutching a thick plaid flannel shirt and a fleece pullover.

"You'll have to roll up the sleeves," he said, handing the bundle to her. "Here, let me help you."

"No, I've got it." She took an involuntary step away from him as she pulled on the shirt, turning the cuffs up several times. It hung to her knees, but the soft, thick fabric would protect her from the chill. She pulled the jacket over her head and zipped the collar up to her neck.

"Cozy?" he asked, looking at her.

She nodded. "Thanks."

The flannel and fleece weren't the only reason the clothes provided welcome warmth.

His scent clung to the fabric, surrounding her like a pair of strong, protective arms.

As she trudged out into the snow behind the others, she breathed in deeply, savoring the sensation of being enveloped in Max's very essence, and knowing this was as close as she could get to the real thing.

* * *

It was snowing in earnest by the time they returned to the cottage after a long walk in the woods. They had seen countless deer but not the moose Sam had promised T.J., though the two boys had found what they claimed were the tracks of a polar bear but more likely belonged to a coyote. Max and Olivia had exchanged amused smiles when the boys shouted that they'd glimpsed the bear up ahead, disappearing into the trees, and had nipped in the bud an enthusiastically hatched plan to track the animal to its "polar bear hideout."

"Mom, look at our car! It's buried," T.J. shouted in glee as they emerged from the trees at the edge of the driveway. "Maybe we're snowbound here."

"Yeah, can they stay, Dad?" Sam asked hopefully, turning to Max. "They'll never get their car out today. Look how hard it's still coming down."

"Of course we can get it out. They're not snowbound," Max said, trying not to sound as wistful as he felt.

He didn't want Olivia to leave.

It felt right to have her here, her and T.J.

The kid was a real charmer—so sweetly naive and looking so much like her that he couldn't possibly have inherited any of his father's features.

Max's thoughts had kept returning to her late husband as they walked, and he couldn't help wondering if what she had told him was all there was to the story.

She'd had a lousy marriage, and her husband had died.

And?

There had to be more to it.

That alone wasn't enough to place the perpetually haunted, frightened expression in her eyes . . . was it?

He, too, had had a mess of a marriage, and his wife had died under the worst possible circumstances he could imagine.

He was weighed down by the past and sobered by it—but frightened?

Threatened?

No.

There was something else, Max knew. Something she wasn't telling him.

Maybe her husband wasn't dead.

It was the only explanation he could think of.

Maybe she had been an abused wife—or maybe the bastard had abused little T.J., too. Maybe she had left him, and was hiding from him.

That would explain a lot of things. Most importantly, it would explain why she didn't want to interact with anyone around here and didn't want them prying into her past.

It would also explain why she had been so skittish about Max's kiss.

Then again, he *had* been out of line, kissing her like that. They barely knew each other.

He had taken advantage of a flicker of intimacy, unable to help himself. She must have been startled, and he could hardly blame her for that.

But . . .

She had kissed him back.

That hadn't been his imagination. No, he knew she had kissed him as though she wanted him as badly as he wanted her.

As he watched her good-naturedly bend to tuck the bottoms of T.J.'s pants into his boots for the umpteenth time, he told himself again that he would never have her.

But this time, for the first time, his inner voice wasn't very convincing.

And with that realization, a small ember of hope ignited.

Max wondered if—

It was out of the question that he would allow himself to fall in love with Olivia.

No, *love* couldn't possibly happen. There were too many risks involved with that.

But what could possibly be wrong with . . .

Well, with a *fling*?

He hated the word, hated the implications, but it was the most harmless, least degrading label he could think of for what he wanted to do with Olivia Halloran.

He wanted to make love to her, without strings.

He *needed* to make love to her.

They were both battle-scarred, both lonely.

And, thank God, she wasn't in the market for marriage any more than he was.

Besides, the attraction between them was growing more palpable by the second. As they had walked through the woods, he kept catching her flashing sidelong glances in his direction.

Whenever he caught her, she looked shyly away; but she knew he had seen her looking. He would be blind not to know what those looks meant.

She was so damned adorable in his oversized clothes. The cold air had put a glow on her usually pale cheeks, and she was laughing at something one of the kids was saying. She looked young and carefree, and he knew this was the perfect time to convince her to come inside again, before she realized that the afternoon was giving way to dusk and she and T.J. should be getting home.

"Come inside and have some of the chili I made last night," he said spontaneously, boldly, touching her sleeve as the children danced around trying to catch the rapidly falling flakes on their tongues.

"Chili? Oh, we can't . . . We have to get back."

"Why? You must be starved. I know I am."

Starved for you, he thought, fighting to keep his eyes

from drifting to her lips. *I want to kiss you again. Right here. Right now. If the kids weren't here . . .*

"All right," she said unexpectedly after casting a glance at T.J., who was merrily ducking a snowball Sam had tossed. "We'll come in for a little while. T.J. loves chili."

"I make the best," he said, breaking into a grin. He couldn't help it.

Right now, his life was as perfect as it had been in a long, long time.

Maybe ever.

And all because of her.

SEVEN

Max never intended to strand her there, in his house, overnight.

No, he merely wanted her to come inside awhile longer so he could get to know her better and continue breaking down the barriers she had so painstakingly constructed.

It wasn't until they were cleaning up the dishes after a lively feast of chili with cheddar cheese and tortilla chips that he glanced out the window over the sink and blinked.

"What's the matter?" Olivia asked beside him, clutching a dish towel and the wet platter he'd just handed her. The kids were busy feeding Lady bits of tortilla chips over by the table.

"Can you flip off that light switch for a minute?" he asked, motioning to the panel a few feet from her hand.

She reached over and the kitchen was plunged into darkness.

Startled, the kids began talking all at once and the dog responded with nervous barks.

With the glare from the inside light gone, Max stared out the window at the solid screen of white. The snow was coming down so hard he couldn't see the outline of the trees or clothesline that were just feet from the glass.

"Oh, my God," Olivia said, beside him.

"It's a real snowstorm," he told her. "You can't go out in this."

"But I have to. I have to get T.J. home. We'll just wait until it lets up. I'm sure it won't be long."

"This looks like the kind of storm that has staying power, Olivia. I haven't heard the weather forecast in a few days—"

"I haven't either."

They looked at each other. He could just make out her expression in the darkened kitchen. It was one of dismay.

"You'll have to stay here," he said, trying his best not to sound delighted.

The kids erupted into joyous shouts nearby, obviously having overheard.

Olivia turned the light back on.

"We can't stay here."

"You have to. You'll never get your car through this kind of snow."

"But . . . can't you drive us home in your truck?"

"No," he said firmly. "I can't take the kids out in this, and you shouldn't, either. The safest thing to do is wait it out here."

"But . . . how long do you think it's going to last?"

"I have no idea."

"Oh."

"T.J. can borrow Sam's pajamas—" He finished drying the big chili pot. "And he can use one of the sleeping bags on the floor of the loft."

"Mmm." She looked distracted.

"I'm sure I can find something of mine for you to wear, and you can have my bed. I'll sleep on the couch," he added hastily when she flashed him a startled look. He leaned past her to put the pot into the cupboard, and his arm brushed against hers.

"Oh," she said, jumping back a little. "That's all right.

You don't have to give up your bed. I can sleep on the couch . . . if it comes to that. I really think this is going to let up."

"I hope so," he said, fervently thinking the opposite. "But until it's clear, you can't go out in the storm. And even after the snow stops, it'll be awhile before you can get out."

"You have a plow for your truck, don't you?"

"I can do the driveway, but you must know how they are about clearing the roads around here. Nobody wanted to approve the increased snow-removal budget I proposed back when I was in office, and it hasn't been picked up since."

"How long do you think we're going to be stuck here?" she looked alarmed.

"At least overnight, Olivia. But as I said, don't worry. We'll take care of sleeping arrangements for you and T.J. and—"

"I'm not worried," she interrupted. "Just a little—surprised. I mean, if I had expected this to happen—why didn't I check the weather report?"

He shrugged. "It's no big deal, Olivia. Relax. How about some hot chocolate?"

He'd said it for the kids' benefit as well, and of course they jumped all over the suggestion. He sent them into the living room and busied himself taking out the milk and finding cocoa powder in the cupboard.

"Can you grab the sugar canister from the counter?" he asked her.

"Don't you use a mix for hot chocolate?"

"No. A mix is no good."

She looked surprised, and impressed, as she handed him the canister. She sat at the table, watching him.

Sarah had taught him to make real hot cocoa. She said those convenience mixes were worthless, and she was right. The bland reconstituted powder couldn't compare to the intense, rich flavor of real hot chocolate.

In his father's house, those packages of instant cocoa were the only kind he had ever had as a kid—when Jack remembered to get groceries at all.

He didn't want Lindsey and Sam to go through that. As he stirred the sugar and cocoa powder together in the pan, he listened to his children's happy voices in the living room. The twins always had a good time together, but the added company of T.J. made it sound like a party.

Much as he wanted to protect them, he'd been wrong to keep them away from other kids. And he was pretty sure Olivia's intentions for T.J. had been the same—to protect him. From what, he wasn't sure. But could it really be necessary for her to isolate the two of them the way she had? As far as he knew, she didn't have a single friend or family member around.

"Is there anyone you should call?" he asked, trying to sound casual.

"Call?" she echoed.

"You know—to say where you are tonight. Is there anyone who'll be worried?"

He turned to look at her and saw that she seemed hesitant. When she said, "No, there's no one," he thought he heard a note of regret in her voice.

"Now that your husband's gone, you and T.J. are alone in the world, aren't you, Olivia?"

She flinched visibly at his words, but didn't deny them. Nor did she speak.

"There's no family, on either side?" he pressed, feeling brazen. "No grandparents for T.J.?"

"I have a stepmother," she said. "But we've never been close. She never even called me back after I let her know that T.J. had been born."

"What about your real parents?"

She took a deep breath. "My mother died when I was a teenager. Skin cancer. She was your typical Southern California sun-worshiper, and she paid the price—at least, that's what my stepmother used to tell me."

"How sympathetic."

She gave a brittle laugh. "Exactly. If you ask me, she had her eye on dad the moment she found out my mother was sick. She was one of our neighbors. My father married her less than a year after Mom died—and I tried not to blame him. He was so lonely. And I had my own life. School, cheerleading, a part-time job at the Gap."

"A boyfriend?" Max asked, curiosity blatant on his face.

She smiled. "Quite a few. Anyway, I was glad there was someone around to look out for Dad. His health wasn't good after he lost Mom. He'd always had asthma. She was the one who reminded him to take his medication, to take it easy when he felt like exerting himself moving furniture around or cleaning out the garage . . ." She shook her head, remembering.

"Anyway," she said, taking a deep breath and continuing matter-of-factly, "Dad was around to walk me down the aisle. He'd always said he wanted to do that. But then, out of the blue, he had a severe asthma attack and died while I was pregnant with T.J."

"God, Olivia, that's terrible. You lost both your parents so young . . ."

Just as he had.

She nodded.

"What about your husband's family? Aren't you in touch with them?"

"No," she said quickly. "Not anymore. They . . . they never took much of an interest in T.J."

He knew he wasn't imagining the high, wavering tone in her voice. She was nervous again.

He dropped the subject of her past, instead asking her

whether she liked her cocoa with whipped cream or marshmallows.

"Don't tell me you're going to whip some heavy cream yourself," she said, smiling faintly.

He was glad that the distraction had worked.

"I wish. Actually, I keep Cool Whip in the freezer for emergencies."

"I'll have some, then. Marshmallows, too."

He grinned. "My pleasure. In fact"—he stretched and reached into the cupboard high above the sink, taking down a bottle—"how about if I add a little of this for us after I fix the kids' cups?"

"What is it?"

"Kahlua. Ever have it in hot chocolate?" He poured the steaming cocoa into three cups for the kids.

She shook her head.

He fully expected her to demur, but she merely watched as he poured the liquor into two more cups. He was generous with it, not wanting to get her drunk, but thinking it wouldn't be a bad thing if she relaxed and forgot her troubles for a while.

He knew he wouldn't mind loosening up a bit. He was growing tense from having to watch everything he said for fear of sending her fleeing into the snow.

"I'll set the kids up with a video upstairs," he said. "I promised Lindsey they could watch *The Lion King* tonight."

"Can't they watch it down here?"

He shook his head. "I put the VCR and television up in their room. I never watch it myself."

"No? What do you do at night, after they're in bed?"

"Read. Work on the house. Listen to music."

"What kind of music?"

"Rock. Jazz. Classical."

"Really?" She looked intrigued. "What do you like to read?"

"I'm working my way through the classics—the stuff I never read when I was supposed to, in high school and college. Whenever I was assigned a book or play, I used to get those yellow Cliffs Notes and skim through so I could write my paper or pass the essay test or whatever. Now I'm kicking myself. I had no idea what I'd missed."

She was smiling, nodding, again looking impressed.

So he'd proven—unexpectedly, from the look on her face—that he was no Neanderthal. Good. One more point in his favor.

"Do you like to read?" he asked her.

She nodded enthusiastically and told him about the literary novel she'd just finished—one that was supposed to be the best book published this year, according to several critics.

"I just didn't get it," she said candidly.

He, too, had read the book—and didn't get it either. He told her so. She looked relieved. They discussed it, and ended up laughing over it.

Then he remembered the hot cocoa for the kids. "I'll get them set upstairs," he said, and handed her a mug of the steaming beverage laced with Kahlua. "Make yourself comfortable in the living room. I'll be right back."

As he herded the three kids up the stairs, he found himself whistling cheerfully. He couldn't help thinking that her walls were tumbling down like dominoes now. With any luck at all, the next time he kissed her, she wouldn't run away.

Even if she wanted to . . . there was nowhere to go.

I don't know what you're so afraid of, Olivia, he thought to himself. *But I won't hurt you. I promise. I'm one of the good guys, and I'm going to prove it.*

* * *

Olivia looked up as Max came down the steps.

"They're all asleep," he said, glancing at the clock above the mantel.

She followed his gaze. Was it really almost midnight? Had they been sitting here talking for hours?

Maybe, she realized, thinking back on all the topics they had covered. They'd started with books, moved on to music, and from there to old movies. Neither of them had seen anything recently. He'd suggested that they might leave all three children with Sarah sometime and catch the new Tom Hanks movie, just so they wouldn't be so out of it.

She'd laughed it off, but was surprised to find how tempting an idea it was.

A movie date? With Max? The very thought of it sent shivers of excitement down her spine. How long had it been since she'd gone out at night, or without T.J.? How long had it been since she'd had a date?

It seemed like another lifetime.

He threw another log on the fire and poked it with a black wrought-iron poker, sending a shower of sparks into the air.

She leaned back on the comfortable couch, watching him.

He put the poker aside and turned to her.

"Tired?"

She shrugged. "Not really. I thought the Kahlua might put me to sleep but I feel energized."

"Well, whenever you're sleepy, tell me and I'll fix up the bed in the other room for you. I just want to find some fresh sheets and clean up the room a little."

"You don't have to do that. Anyway, I told you, I'll sleep on the couch."

"No way. It's narrow. You'll be uncomfortable."

"So will you."

"But you're the guest."

"Not one you were expecting," she pointed out.

"No, but I'm glad you're here."

He sat on the couch again, beside her. He had been in the very same spot only minutes ago, before he'd gone up to check on the kids. Then, when they were engaged in animated conversation, his close proximity hadn't seemed uncomfortably intimate.

Now, amidst the talk of sleeping arrangements, it did.

She fought the urge to move away. If she did, she'd be up against the arm, and she didn't want to seem skittish.

She didn't want him to know how rattled she was by his presence—that she could think of nothing but what it would be like to be in those arms, to feel him wrapped around her.

The thought had been in the back of her mind all night—all day, really.

How could she forget that kiss that had caught her so off guard the other day?

How could she ignore the possibility that he might do it again, at any time?

How could she ignore the unsettling truth that she *wanted* him to do it again?

No sooner had the thought crossed her mind than he leaned closer to her. She barely had time to marvel at the fact that he'd once again read her mind before his mouth came down over hers.

It was as though years of pent up emotion and frustration—hers, and his—were released in that kiss.

His tongue was in her mouth and her hands were on the back of his head, pulling him closer, and she knew that she could never get enough of him. Not this way.

Gone was any shred of restraint; any reminder of the past; any fear of future repercussions.

There was only here and now, and this was right.

Olivia moaned when his hands moved over the big flannel shirt she still wore. He fumbled with the buttons, then gave up and burrowed underneath, lifting that and her tee shirt so that his fingers were on her bare skin.

She shivered at the contact, and leaned back to give him better access as he moved deftly to the front hook of her bra. When it was loosened and his hands found her bare breasts, she gasped sharply at the exquisite pleasure of being touched this way, by this man.

"Did I hurt you?" he lifted his head from her mouth to ask.

"No," she said. "God, no. It's just . . ."

He lowered his head again, this time closing his lips over one taut nipple, and she moaned, the words snatched from her mind. She couldn't think, could only feel. He nuzzled first one breast and then the other, his hands stroking her stomach, her hips, her legs—everyplace but the most sensitive spot that ached for him most. Her nipples were tingling and wet from his mouth and there was a pressure building at her core, and she writhed on the couch, needing more still.

"Max," she gasped when she could no longer stand it.

"Let me make love to you, Olivia."

"Yes . . . now . . ."

"Not here."

And she knew, somewhere in the fog that obscured most rational thought, that he was thinking of the kids. Even the vague reminder that they weren't alone in the house didn't quell her desire. When he stood and pulled her up, she went willingly, following him to the one room she had never seen—his bedroom.

It was dark, and he didn't turn on a light.

"Careful," he said, and she heard him pushing something—a box?—across the floor. "I've been working in here. It's a mess. I don't want you to see it. Just close your eyes and pretend we're in a beautiful meadow . . ." He laughed, and so did she.

They found the bed and he lowered her to the mattress, his weight on top of her. She could feel the hard length of him against her, and she squirmed, needing him to increase the pressure. They were both wearing jeans, and the stiff fabric was a barrier—but only temporarily.

She reached for the top button of her jeans and found his hands there already, unfastening and then unzipping, helping her out of her clothes until she was naked, lying on the bed, waiting.

She heard the soft rustling of fabric as he, too, undressed. Then he lay down beside her, pulling a soft quilt over them both and cradling her in his arms. She expected him to enter her quickly; he must have been as eager and ready as she was. Instead, as though they had all the time in the world, he kissed her again, deeply. His hands stroked her gently, every part of her, languidly working their way down to the apex of her legs, where she knew his mere touch would send her over the edge.

He avoided direct contact, though, running his fingers over her hips and her inner thighs and her lower belly . . . until she thought she would go crazy with need.

Finally, when she gasped his name in a frenzied plea, he yanked open a drawer and she heard the telltale sound of him ripping open a foil packet. In her distracted state she hadn't even thought to worry about protection. Thankful that he had, she told herself she couldn't be this reckless again, not after this. She'd just let herself have this one time with him, and that would be it.

Moments later, all rational thought left her mind as he rolled on top of her and into her in one incredible movement.

She moaned at the sheer intensity of her body's reaction to the invasion. He thrust into her again, and that was all it took to launch, at last, a dizzying explosion within her. She quaked and clung to him and he whispered her name against her ear as he moved inside of her toward a powerful, molten release that came as her own was quieting.

She savored his every quiver, his faintest moan, struck by the amazing realization that *she* had done this to him, that *she* was capable of bringing him to such mind-reeling heights.

"Was that all right?" he asked when he had quieted.

The question was so ludicrous that they both burst into laughter.

"It was all right," she said in a mock-blasé tone. "Maybe you can do better next time."

"There's going to be a next time?" he asked, tenderly petting her hair.

"Isn't there?" she hardly dared ask as a pinprick of misgiving threatened to deflate her elation. She had told herself it would be just this once—

No, don't think . . . Not now. Don't stop to think, she commanded herself.

Tonight was for her—for them. There was no one else.

"Not for at least ten minutes," he said, so breathlessly that she had to laugh again.

"That long?"

"Okay, five minutes."

She doubted they even waited that long before they were at it again, stroking and tasting and savoring each other, skin to skin, her heart pounding in rhythm with his beneath the warm quilt in the darkened bedroom.

EIGHT

"Good morning . . ."

The voice slammed into Olivia's head, startling her from a deep sleep that, for the first time in years, hadn't been invaded by nightmares.

She opened her eyes.

The first thing she saw was the window beside the bed. There were no shades or blinds. She saw bare branches fringed in white against a milky-gray sky. The storm was over.

She turned her head on the pillow.

Max was standing over her, wearing a soft-looking gray crewneck sweatshirt and faded jeans. His thick, wavy dark hair looked damp, and she could smell the soap-clean scent of his skin.

Slightly dazed, she looked around and realized that she was in his bed, in his very cluttered bedroom, and—when she started to sit up—that she wasn't wearing any clothes beneath the warm quilt. She lay down again, pulling the quilt up to her chin.

Her voice came out husky, the way it always did first thing in the morning. "What's going on? T.J.—"

"Don't worry, he's fine. The kids are in the kitchen, starting their french toast. Oh, and by the way, I slept on the couch."

She stared at him. Did he actually think she didn't remember what they had done last night, well into the wee hours, before falling asleep in each other's arms?

"I know, I know," he said, flashing a conspiratorial grin, "but that's what I told them. Not that they care one way or another. They're full of plans to go polar bear tracking after breakfast."

"Well, as soon as T.J.'s done eating, we've got to go home," she said, wanting to get up but trapped beneath the blanket and his intent gaze.

"You don't have to leave yet, Olivia—"

"Yes, we really do. This is . . ." She trailed off, feeling helpless.

"This is what?"

"Wrong," she said, plucking the first word that entered her mind.

"You mean, because the kids are here?"

"Obviously that's an issue. But beyond that, even . . . what were we thinking? How could we have been so careless?"

He shrugged. "Olivia, stop the guilt. I don't have any regrets about last night. It was something we both wanted—needed. I won't deny that and you shouldn't try."

She said nothing. Her thoughts were racing. She had to get out of here before . . .

Before *what*?

What was going to happen?

She felt the flicker of panic subsiding a bit.

Making love with Max Rothwell might not have been the most prudent thing she could have done, but it hadn't necessarily placed her and T.J. in any immediate jeopardy.

Everything would be fine as long as she got out of here before she found herself letting her guard down further.

Before she went and spilled secrets she couldn't afford to share. As long as he didn't know the truth, no damage had been done.

"Listen, Max," she said, weighing her words carefully, forcing herself to look him in the eye, "You're right. What happened between us was—well, I guess it was inevitable. You're lonely; I'm lonely—but that doesn't mean that it's exactly a good idea to prolong . . ."

She paused, waiting for him to voice his agreement.

Instead, he said, "Prolong what?"

"You know . . . my leaving. Our keeping a safe distance from each other so that—well, so that this won't happen again."

"Not that I have any immediate plans," he said, shifting his weight and folding his arms across his broad chest, "But . . . why can't it happen again?"

"Because!" she said, as though that alone were a sufficient explanation. She faltered, then elaborated. "Neither of us wants anything . . . permanent."

He nodded. "Go on."

"So . . . seeing each other again might just tempt us to—I don't know—to think we can actually have some kind of relationship when there's just no way."

She waited for a response.

He said nothing, but seemed to be waiting, too.

Why wouldn't he help her out here? Why did he have to make this so difficult?

She plunged on. "I mean, I know you're not interested in getting married again—"

"No," he said, so quickly and forcefully that she blinked, taken aback.

Okay, so the mention of marriage had gotten him talking.

And he had made his intentions loud and clear with that forceful one-word response.

He was looking for a good time. Nothing more. He thought they could sleep together with no strings attached, until they got this crazy attraction out of their systems. Was that it?

Anger sizzled through her and she realized she resented him for that attitude . . . which was insane. After all, she didn't want anything more than sex from him, did she?

Hell, she didn't even want that. She didn't want to sleep with him again. It was too risky.

If she slept with him again, she might be tempted to want more—even if he so obviously didn't.

"So, you don't want to get married," she said, trying to keep the brittle tone from her voice, not wanting him to suspect he had riled her, "and I don't, either. So, what's the point of seeing each other again?"

"I don't think we can avoid it. The kids . . . remember? We agreed they should be friends. It's not fair to penalize them just because we can't get along like responsible adults."

"Fine. So our kids will play together sometimes. I'll drop T.J. off; I'll pick him up . . . it doesn't mean we have to sleep together, Max."

"No. You're right."

His eyes flicked over the length of her, and she fought the urge to squirm. It was as though he could see right through the blanket. She remembered how he had run his hands over her naked body, the things he had done to her, and she felt embers stirring at her core.

"Do you have something I can wear so I can go take a shower?" she asked abruptly.

She knew she couldn't put her clothes on again without washing away the remnants of what they had done last night. She could smell his scent on her skin, in her hair.

"Sure." He tossed her a thick navy velour robe, a tee

shirt, and some thermal-knit long underwear. "Put these on. But come eat breakfast first. You have to come through the kitchen to get to the bathroom anyway, and everything's ready. The kids are waiting for you."

She hesitated, wanting to tell him she couldn't do something like that—sit down and eat french toast with him and the kids, as though they were all a big happy family. No, she shouldn't linger a moment longer than was necessary.

But, somehow, the words wouldn't come.

She wanted to eat breakfast in that cozy kitchen of his, dammit. Just as they had eaten dinner last night, the five of them gathered around the table, laughing and talking the way families did.

She was hungry for french toast, hungry for the company, for the illusion that she and T.J. weren't utterly alone in the world. Just this one last time. And then she'd leave, and she'd never come back. Not if she could help it.

She would find T.J. some other friends if she had to. She'd do whatever it took to keep from having to see Max Rothwell and his two motherless children ever again.

"More coffee?"

Olivia shook her head, having just pushed her chair away from the table. "I really should go."

Max picked up the coffeepot in one hand and the cobalt-blue mug in the other. "Just have a little more. It'll warm you up before you go out there."

"Max, I've got to go. You promised to plow me out."

"I know, I know . . ." He put another piece of the golden egg-rich french toast on his plate and smothered it in maple syrup. It was his third helping. "I'll do that just as soon as I'm done eating."

Looking bemused, she stared as he put a big forkful into his mouth. Then, slowly, she pulled her chair closer to the table again and picked up her mug, taking a sip.

He noticed that although she'd barely touched her own french toast when they'd first sat down, her plate was now empty. She couldn't stay silent and unsmiling long with the three kids chattering away around them. Even after the kids had gone outside to shovel the step and walk, Olivia had seemed caught up in the conversation Max kept going.

He'd told her stories about things he and Andy had done when they were young—how he had once fallen through the ice in the pond while they were skating and Andy pulled him out and how they had once tried to dig their way to China through Sarah's petunia patch, which hadn't gone over well with her.

Now, he saw the remnants of laughter in Olivia's eyes, and he struggled to think of something to say that would keep her here, keep her laughing, keep her from saying that they shouldn't see each other again . . . even though he knew she was right. It would be best for them to stay away from each other.

When it came right down to it, he didn't think they could be together without falling into bed again at the first opportunity. Last night had been too good. Too addicting.

If it happened again, he might fall in love. If he fell in love, he might want to marry her. If he married her, she might leave.

He couldn't go through that again.

He couldn't put his children through it again.

Olivia isn't Julia.

The thought ran through his mind again, as it had since he had awakened to find her sleeping in his arms.

Olivia didn't seem capable of hurting him—hurting anyone—the way Julia had.

Yet . . .

She was hiding something from him. And he couldn't help suspecting that where there were secrets, there were lies.

So. It would be best if she left.

This time, when she put down her mug and pushed her chair away from the table, he didn't stop her.

No, he plowed the driveway while she was in the shower and he dusted off her car and started it for her so that it would be warm. He gave T.J. a plastic bag full of Sarah's cookies to take home, and when Sam and Lindsey asked him, in front of Olivia, when T.J. and Olivia could come over again, he pretended not to hear. So did she.

And then she was driving off down the snowy lane through the trees and he and his children were left alone again—just as they had been for years, really. Just the way he wanted it.

But suddenly, the house felt empty and quiet.

Max wondered if he had made a mistake.

Maybe so.

But he couldn't think of any way to change things. This was how it had to be. The sooner he forgot Olivia Halloran existed, the better.

"Here, Olivia, why don't you start unwrapping this china while I sort through the children's clothes?" Amy said, shoving a big box in Olivia's direction across the concrete floor of the garage.

"Where should I put it?" Olivia asked, surveying the mounds of newspaper-wrapped dishes and cups. The garage was already overflowing with what appeared to be mostly junk, although Lisa had found a bunch of old Partridge Family albums that she had to have and Amy laid claim to a pile of outdated cross-stitch magazines.

"If you see anything you want, Olivia, you should take it," Amy kept saying as Olivia sorted through bags of worn clothes.

Actually, she could use some new things, and so could T.J., but she wasn't in the mood to think about that now.

It seemed she wasn't in the mood, lately, to think about anything but Max.

Her thoughts drifted to him as she began unwrapping one saucer after another, idly noting that the china was an ugly blue-and-brown pattern and wondering who would ever have bought such a thing in the first place.

Would she ever see Max again?

What if she didn't?

How could she last a lifetime without seeing him when every day since she'd left his house had seemed endless?

She had tried, unsuccessfully, to come up with some way to work things out with him—some way that they could have a relationship without getting involved in any of the tricky stuff.

Like emotions.

It was no use. No matter how she figured it, seeing Max again meant only one thing: getting hurt.

She had to steer clear.

Which should be relatively easy, considering that he had made no attempt to see her.

Apparently, he'd decided she was right; and for that, she should be grateful. She was fairly positive that she could never resist him if he showed up at her door and begged her to see him again.

"Anything good in there?"

Olivia jumped.

Lisa had come up behind her and was peering over her shoulder into the box of china.

"Not really," Olivia said. "The pattern isn't very—"

"Ick!" Lisa said, picking up a saucer and examining it. "Who would buy something like this?"

Olivia smiled. "That's what I was wondering," she admitted. She allowed herself to relax a bit, to push Max from her mind as Lisa told her all about her own set of china, which she and her husband had gotten as a wedding gift. When they split up, according to the divorce agreement, he got the cups and saucers, she got the plates and bowls.

"Isn't that the stupidest thing you ever heard?" Lisa asked. "I mean, who wants half a set of china? I figured he'd let me have all of it, since he never liked the pattern in the first place. But the bastard took every cup and saucer, and I even caught him trying to sneak the gravy boat out of the breakfront. So, I told him that if he took the gravy boat; I would take his golf clubs. I mean, why does he need a gravy boat? He doesn't even know how to make gravy. His idea of making dinner is putting a packet of ketchup on his McDonald's fries."

Olivia found herself smiling as she unwrapped another piece.

"Oh, hey, look at this," Lisa said, plucking the plate out of her hand. This was a different pattern—plain white with a raised floral border. "This stuff is nice. Is there any more of it in there?"

"I don't know." Olivia peeked into the carton.

As she glanced over the other pieces, a yellowed photo on one of the crumpled pieces of packing newspaper caught her eye.

Her heart stopped.

It was a photo she had seen before, of T.J. as an infant. She'd had it taken herself, at J.C. Penney, just before his first Christmas. It was the same photo she had seen on the milk carton in the supermarket before they came to Newberry Cove.

Accompanying the photo of T.J. was a snapshot of a woman who looked nothing like Olivia, unless someone looked at it very closely.

She snatched the paper from the box, hoping Lisa hadn't noticed it. But she had forgotten the paper was wrapped around a plate, and it fell to the floor and shattered at her feet.

"Hey, what are you doing?" Lisa asked, jumping back and looking at Olivia as if she'd lost her mind.

"Nothing, I just—"

"Why'd you grab it like that? I wasn't going to steal it out from under you. Jeez!"

Mortified, her heart pounding in terror, Olivia said nothing, just clutched the piece of newspaper and stared at the broken plate on the floor.

Amy, too, had come over to see what was going on.

"I'll get a broom," she said, shooting a puzzled look at Olivia. "Throw that paper away—will you?—and grab the dustpan."

Olivia didn't move, clinging to the piece of newspaper, using every bit of willpower to keep from fleeing the garage and their curious stares.

If she did that, they would label her a nut, and she wouldn't blame them. She had to play it cool.

Her fingers trembled as she crumpled the piece of newspaper and tossed it into the box where she had thrown the rest of it. She tried to act casual about it and took the dustpan Amy handed her.

As she bent to hold it at an angle against the floor so that Amy could sweep the shards of broken glass into it, she saw Lisa out of the corner of her eye, going over to the box of newspaper.

She knows I saw something in the paper, she thought, frantic. She's trying to see what it was that startled me that way.

She watched furtively as Lisa picked up the wad of paper, glanced over it and then at Olivia.

She didn't dare meet her gaze head-on, but she could almost feel the wheels working in her mind.

She recognizes me, Olivia thought, her heart sinking. *Any second now, she's going to accuse me of—*

"Olivia," Lisa said, tossing the paper back into the box and turning back to the carton of china, "if you don't want this floral-patterned stuff, you don't mind if I take it, do you?"

Olivia nearly sobbed in relief. "No," she said, struggling to sound just as casual as she straightened and carried the full dustpan over to the garbage can. "Go ahead. Take it."

But long after the three of them had resumed their unpacking and sorting, she thought she felt Lisa's eyes on her, scrutinizing her.

Was it her imagination?

Or had Lisa realized that T.J. was the missing child in the picture—and Olivia was wanted for kidnapping her own son? There was no way of knowing.

When everything was unpacked and dusk had fallen outside, Amy said, "I guess we should call it a day. I can finish the last few things later on."

Olivia was partly grateful that she could make her escape, but she couldn't leave that newspaper behind. She had been waiting for an opportunity to snatch it from the box, but it was now buried beneath piles of rumpled newspaper and there was no way she could dig it out without arousing suspicion.

There was nothing to do but leave, and tell herself that she was only imagining Lisa's wary gaze following her.

Max looked up from the wood he was chopping, startled at the unexpected sound of car tires crunching down the long, winding driveway. In the split second before the vehicle came into view, he realized who it was.

Olivia.

She must have spent the past few endless days and sleepless nights just as he had—consumed by memories of what had happened between them. Only she had come to her senses before him and was making the first move.

His heart leapt in anticipation and he plunged the axe into the log and left it there as he turned to greet her.

Just as quickly as his hopes had risen, they plummeted to the soles of his Timberlands. The car pulling up in front of his house didn't belong to Olivia. It was a familiar blue-and-white police cruiser, and his friend Andy Polucci was behind the wheel.

For once, an unexpected visit from Andy didn't jab Max's heart with a finger of dread. He knew the kids were safe; he had just left them in the living room, where they were optimistically teaching a sleepy Lady how to sit up and beg.

Max tried hard to look pleased to see Andy, concealing his disappointment behind a cheerful grin.

"What brings you all the way out here in the middle of a workday?" he asked when Andy had parked and gotten out of the car.

"My wife."

"Janey's with you?" Max peered into the car and saw that it was empty.

"Nope. She's home with the kids, probably watching that *Blue's Clues* show again. It's all the boys ever want to watch. Sam and Lindsey into that?"

Max shook his head. "We don't have cable. They mostly watch Disney videos."

"Count yourself lucky. Janey said to invite you and the kids over for Thanksgiving dinner next week."

"You came all the way out here to invite me for Thanksgiving? Why didn't you just call?"

"Because Janey wanted me to bring you this." Andy reached into the back seat and took out a foil-covered casserole dish. "It's that chicken-and-rice thing with the vegetables that she made when you came for dinner last month."

"The kids loved it." Max took the dish and held it carefully level. "Thanks, Andy."

"It's no problem. Janey thinks that none of you Rothwells are eating anything but Spaghetti-o's. She said you need some home cooking."

"Well, between her and your mother, we're actually quite well-fed." Max smiled, trying not to show the vague sense of discomfort that had overtaken him.

Why was Janey Polucci's gesture bothering him? He never minded when she and Sarah sent over food. In fact, he always appreciated it.

But today, he felt acutely aware that his family was sorely incomplete. He didn't have a wife; the kids didn't have a mother. Covered casseroles and holidays spent with friends' families couldn't possibly make up for what was missing in the Rothwells' lives.

He needed a wife.

The kids needed a mother.

"No!"

"What's that, Max?"

He hadn't realized he'd blurted it aloud until he heard Andy's question.

"Oh . . . nothing. I guess my mind wandered." He frowned.

"Anything bothering you, Max?"

"Nope.

"My mother said the kids told her about your friends. Olivia and T.J."

"Oh. Yeah, they would tell her about that." Lately the Hallorans were all Sam and Lindsey talked about.

"What about it?"

"What did your mother tell you?"

"Just that you have some new friends and that one is the most beautiful lady the kids have ever seen. They said she's the angel who rescued them from the water."

"Right."

"So?"

Max scowled. "So, what?"

"What's going on, Max? You going back on your word to stay away from women?"

Max fully intended to deny Andy's insinuation, but somehow, he couldn't. Andy knew him too well and was watching him too carefully.

Besides, the subject of Olivia was too emotionally raw to be brushed off with casual denial.

"Yeah, Andy, I guess I did go back on my word," Max admitted, picking up the axe again. He swung it and plunged it into the wood with a dull, satisfying cracking sound.

"So, what's going on with her?"

"Nothing. That's the problem. Neither one of us wants any kind of relationship. It's the kids—"

"Yours?"

"And hers. He's a good little kid, T.J. Seems so lonely. I get the feeling he could use a father figure—"

"And you don't want it to be you?"

"Yeah. That, and some other stuff."

"About her? What?"

Max hesitated. This time, something made him shrug and say, "Nothing I want to talk about."

That was the truth. He didn't want to tell Andy that Olivia was clearly hiding something.

After all, Andy was a law-enforcement official. If someone was acting suspiciously, he would be duty-bound to check it out. The last thing Max wanted to do was send the police snooping around Olivia. He knew how she'd react to that.

But what if she's on the lam? What if she's done something illegal and there's a warrant for her arrest? That would explain why she's so paranoid and so damn private . . .

But even if there were a distinct possibility that Olivia was in trouble with the law, Max couldn't bring himself to believe she deserved to be reported. His gut instincts told him to protect her at any cost, not to turn her in.

"You sure you don't want to get things off your chest?" Andy asked, still watching him carefully.

"Yeah, I'm sure." He swung the axe again, then paused to ask, "You want to come in for some coffee? A beer?"

"No, thanks. I'm on the job. Gotta get going. Janey said to heat that casserole on three-fifty for an hour."

"I'll do that. Thank her for me, Andy."

"I will." Andy hesitated with his hand on the car-door handle. "You know, Max, not every woman is Julia. In fact, most aren't."

Max was silent.

"You can't let her stop you from ever having a life, Max."

"I have a life."

"Okay, then a wife. You don't have a wife."

"No. I don't have a wife. I had a wife. I don't need another one."

He swung the axe hard. Hit the wood. Swung again. Hit it again.

Then he left it there and looked at Andy. "Trouble is, I'll never be sure the next woman I meet doesn't have a Julia lurking somewhere deep down inside."

"Mmm-hmm. Well, one thing's for certain."

"What's that?"

"Julia would never have jumped into the frigid ocean and dragged out her own two kids, Max—let alone somebody else's. Think about it."

With that, Andy waved, got into the police cruiser, and drove away.

"I *am* thinking about it," Max muttered, picking up the axe again. "That's the problem."

Olivia spent the next forty-eight hours imagining that Lisa had recognized her and it was only a matter of time before the authorities came knocking on her door to arrest her.

The only good thing about that was that it took her mind off Max.

Almost.

He still invaded her thoughts every now and then, the image of his ruggedly handsome face and the memory of being cradled in his arms serving only as harsh reminders of what would never be.

T.J. asked several times about seeing Sam and Lindsey, but she kept putting him off, hoping he would give up—though she knew that was unlikely.

Late Friday afternoon, when the early November dusk had lengthened shadows outside the veterinary clinic, Dr. Klimek left to visit a neighboring farm where a laboring horse had run into trouble.

He offered to take T.J. with him, but something made Olivia say no.

"Come on, Mom," T.J. said, anxiously looking up from the homework he was doing at a table in the waiting room. "It's so boring here. Let me go."

"Not today," Olivia said, so sharply that both T.J. and the old doctor looked startled.

"Why not?"

"Because you have homework to do, that's why. And it's going to snow later."

"So? It snows all the time."

"They're predicting a big storm this weekend, and it's going to start tonight."

"Mom—"

"No. Now stop bugging me."

She walked over to the door after Dr. Klimek had closed it behind him and driven away. Peering through the window, she saw that the parking lot was empty.

For some reason, she was feeling uneasy.

True, she hadn't exactly been able to relax since the incident in Amy's garage on Wednesday afternoon. But instead of fading with time, her fear that she'd been discovered was growing stronger.

Restless, she wandered back over to the desk and picked up the pile of bills she'd been sorting. She was aware of the silence as she worked, hearing only T.J.'s pencil scratching on his homework paper and the wind rustling in the trees outside.

Maybe the storm was already kicking up, she thought. She'd heard on the radio that this was going to be a bad one.

The sudden ringing of the telephone made her jump and gasp.

T.J. looked up at her, apparently more startled by her reaction than by the phone.

"Geez, Mom, it's just the telephone. Aren't you going to get it?"

"Of course I'm going to get it," she said, pressing a hand against her wildly beating heart.

She picked up the receiver before it could ring again and said, in her usual professional voice, "Dr. Klimek's office, how may I help you?"

"Katie?"

She froze.

For a moment, she believed that it was a wrong number.

That the raspy male voice belonged to some innocent caller who was looking for someone else.

Not for Olivia Halloran, who, before she'd taken her son and run for their lives, had once been named Katie.

Katie Kenrick . . .

"Is that you, Katie?"

There was a chuckle on the other end of the line.

And then she knew.

"How are you? How's little Tommy?"

She whimpered and threw the receiver down.

"Mom?" T.J. was watching her, fear in his eyes.

She couldn't find her voice.

"What's wrong, Mom? Who was it?"

"We've got to get out of here, T.J.," she said, already grabbing him by the arm.

"Huh? Where are we going?"

"I don't know. We just have to—we have to go."

"What's going on, Mom?"

She couldn't reply. She shoved his coat at him as she slipped her arms into the sleeves of her own, then pulled him to the door.

It was too late.

She saw the arc of headlights swinging into the parking lot, and realized that it wasn't Dr. Klimek's car.

This was a sport utility vehicle, and she saw the silhouette of a man behind the wheel.

Panic surged through her.

Feeling trapped, she stood in the doorway, clutching T.J.'s shoulders, partly to protect him, partly to support herself so that she wouldn't faint.

She watched the lights draw closer, and then the vehicle came to a stop a few feet from the door.

The engine was running and the bright headlights were shining in Olivia's eyes, blinding her as the driver got out and approached.

She braced herself for the encounter she had dreaded—and, she realized, fully expected—ever since she'd fled California so many years ago.

She tightened her hands on T.J.'s shoulders, telling herself her son wouldn't be taken from her without a fight.

He'd have to kill her to get to T.J.—that was the only way she'd give him up.

"Olivia?"

She flinched as he stopped walking, a few feet from her, and she heard her name.

Then reality hit her and she stared in disbelief.

"What's going on? Why are you standing there like that?" He came closer. "Are you all right?"

Weak with relief, she opened her mouth to speak.

She was able to utter only one word.

His name.

"Max . . ."

NINE

"When we get to my place, you're going to tell me what's going on," Max told Olivia firmly as he steered the Explorer over the rutted road leading away from the clinic.

She said nothing.

He clenched his jaw and stared straight ahead through the windshield. He'd had it with her, and yet . . .

A familiar, fierce, protective instinct welled up inside him every time he allowed himself to glance her way.

He deserved to know why she had been huddled in that doorway, her arms wrapped protectively around her son as if she were expecting a rabid animal to leap out of the shadows and attack.

She was going to tell him why she had at first thrown herself into his arms, sobbing, then tried to pull away and claim that nothing was the matter.

When he'd told her, fed up, that he wasn't stupid or blind and that he knew something was wrong, she hadn't argued.

Instead, she'd taken him completely by surprise, asking him if he could bring her and T.J. to his house.

He hadn't bothered to ask why, or for how long.

He wouldn't have dreamed of denying her request, of turning his back on her.

He *couldn't.*

In fact, that was why he'd shown up at the clinic in the first place.

He'd spent too many sleepless nights of late, thinking about her as he lay in his cold, lonely bed. If she'd had a phone he would have called her long before now, his resolve worn down by the all-consuming hunger to see her again and the reminder, after his conversation with Andy the other day, that he and the kids were too damned lonely.

Finally, when he could no longer stand it, Sarah had showed up, as she always did—with orders for him to make himself scarce while she made cupcakes with the children.

Grateful, he found himself heading for the clinic to talk to Olivia in person. Apparently, she had been expecting somebody else.

Somebody who frightened her.

T.J. broke the silence in the car. "Am I going to see Sam and Lindsey at your house, Max?"

"You sure are. Do you like chocolate cupcakes with frosting and sprinkles?"

"Yup."

"Well, the kids should be taking a batch out of the oven right about now." He struggled to keep his voice light and added, for Olivia's benefit, "Sam and Lindsey have been asking about both of you. They'll be glad to have you come for a visit."

She said nothing, just stared out the window on the passenger's side of the Explorer, her body turned away from him, her arms wound around herself as though she were cold or terrified, or both.

He turned up the heat control on the dashboard for something to do, then clicked on the radio. A love song was playing—the Celine Dion theme from the movie *Ti-*

tanic. He'd been sick of this song two years ago. Now he found himself appreciating the lyrics, and feeling hopelessly sappy for the romantic thoughts it inspired. He seemed to have no control over the fantasies that drifted into his mind as he drove. But as long as he could control his feelings . . .

He couldn't let himself fall in love with Olivia Halloran. Why had he gone to the clinic tonight?

Why had he allowed himself to stumble into the tense scenario that was playing itself out in the clinic doorway?

Who the hell was she expecting?

He had a feeling he knew. It was the oldest story in the book. Her husband. She must have lied about his being dead. He was after her.

Well, if that were the case, he would protect her, he thought, bristling at the very idea of some jealous lunatic frightening Olivia enough to have put that permanently haunted, tortured look in her eyes.

Finally, he pulled into his driveway. The cabin came into view among the trees, lamplight spilling from the windows. Most of last week's snow had melted, but there were a few patchy remnants on the grass, like forlorn reminders of their snowbound night together.

He pulled up behind Sarah's white Buick.

"Who's here?" Olivia spoke for the first time, and he turned to see that frantic expression edging onto her face again.

"Sarah. My friend Andy's mother. The one who does all the baking. Remember, I told you about her. She's making cupcakes with the kids."

"Yum," T.J. said, putting his hand on the door handle as Max put the car into park.

"Wait," Olivia blurted.

T.J. turned to look at her in surprise.

So did Max. "What's the matter?"

"I didn't know anyone was here."

"Did you think I left the kids alone?" he asked, unable to keep the sarcasm from his tone. He was angry with her, dammit.

Why did she have to make things so complicated?

"Of course I know you wouldn't leave them alone. I just . . . I'm sorry. I didn't stop to think. I was so preoccupied—"

"And when we get inside and T.J. is settled with the kids, you're going to tell me what it is that has you so upset," Max reminded her, softening his voice.

She looked up at him.

She seemed so young suddenly. Like Lindsey when she was hurting and needed a hug to make it all better.

But Max knew that innocence was an illusion.

She was a grown woman. If he hugged Olivia, it wouldn't end there unless she stopped it, because *he* sure as hell had no self-control when she was in his arms.

"Anything I tell you, if I tell you . . . well, I don't want your friend to know, okay?" she said, her trepidation evident in the way she burrowed into her navy pea coat, hunching her shoulders.

"Look, I won't tell her anything," he said, irked by the *if* she had tacked on. "She can keep an eye on the kids while you and I talk."

She looked hesitant.

"Listen, Olivia, I've known Sarah my whole life. Take my word for it. You can trust her with T.J."

"It's not that . . ."

And he realized what she was thinking. That it was he she wasn't sure if she should trust—about Sarah, or anything else.

How could he convince her that her secret was safe with him?

That she and T.J. were safe with him?

He would never let anything hurt them.

Never, he thought passionately, clenching his jaw as he turned off the engine and opened the door.

"Come on," he said, getting out and helping T.J. out of the back seat. "Let's get inside. It's cold out here."

Still she hesitated.

He walked around to her side of the car and opened her door. She flinched when he reached inside and touched her sleeve.

"Olivia," he said in a low voice. T.J. was already bounding up the front steps. "Let's go inside. It's all right. I won't let anything happen to you."

Her startled gaze met his. "T.J. and I are in danger, Max," she said, a tremble in her voice.

"I know."

"If we come inside—if we involve you—I just can't—"

"Olivia, it's going to be all right. But you need to tell me what's going on. The truth, Olivia."

She bit her lip, then nodded.

Together, they followed T.J. into the house.

Olivia wrapped her hands around the mug of hot tea, letting its warmth seep through her skin, wishing it could somehow erase the chill that had invaded her soul.

He'd found her.

Well, she'd always known he would, hadn't she?

It must have been Lisa.

She must have recognized Olivia and T.J. from those yellowed newspaper photos. She must have called the eight-hundred-number hotline the Murdocks had set up in California.

Olivia had seen it printed beneath the photos; had seen it on the MISSING notice plastered on that milk carton back in the Midwest.

The irony was, Lisa probably thought she was doing the right thing. Olivia couldn't even hate her. In her shoes, she probably would have reacted the same way. She would have thought she was helping an endangered child.

Little did Lisa know she had endangered the child in making her phone call.

"All right. Tell me about your husband."

Max's voice startled her. She had forgotten he was seated beside her on the couch, holding his own mug of the tea which Sarah had fixed for both of them in the kitchen.

She was a nice woman, with twinkling brown eyes and a quick laugh. Olivia had liked her instantly, liked the way she took T.J. under her wing, handing him a can of rainbow-colored sprinkles to shake over the vanilla cupcakes Sam and Lindsey were smearing with chocolate icing.

She liked the way Sarah readily agreed to keep the three children busy in the kitchen while Max and Olivia had an important conversation here in the living room.

She liked the way Sarah had smiled kindly at her, even though she hadn't been in any condition to make friendly small talk.

Sarah didn't seem to be judging her or wondering about her. No, she just poured hot tea from the already-steaming kettle on the stove and she scooted Olivia and Max into the living room and closed the door behind them.

Olivia noticed now that since they'd entered the room a few minutes ago, Max had built a fire on the hearth and turned on soft jazz. The music would drown out anything they said, should anyone in the kitchen try to eavesdrop. Judging by the faint sound of happy laughter coming from the next room, Olivia knew that wasn't likely.

"Olivia?" Max prodded, and she realized he was waiting for her to answer his question.

About her husband.

"My husband?" she repeated. "As I told you, he died about five years ago."

She didn't miss the disappointment in Max's green eyes.

"The truth, Olivia," he said, in a no-nonsense tone that was patient just the same.

"That *is* the truth, Max."

He studied her.

"Why do you think I'm lying?"

"If your husband is dead, then who did you expect to see back there in the parking lot of the clinic?"

She took a deep breath, realizing she could no longer delay spilling the nightmarish tale of her past—and that she no longer wanted to.

She had to tell someone; she had kept it in for so long. And now that her life, and T.J.'s, was in danger, Max was the only person she could count on to help her escape. This time, she couldn't do it alone.

"My husband's brother," she said, looking Max in the eye before she uttered the name she hadn't spoken aloud in years. "Gregory Murdock."

Of course there was no flicker of recognition on Max's face. Why would there be? The Murdock name wouldn't be renowned here, in small-town New England, as it was in Los Angeles.

"Your brother-in-law?" Max asked. "And you're afraid of him."

She nodded.

"Why?"

"It's a long story."

"We've got all night." He leaned back against the cushion, took a sip of tea, and waited.

She fidgeted with the handle of her mug.

The fire crackled.

The mantel clock ticked.

Outside the wind blew. It wasn't snowing yet, but it would be, soon. She shifted on her seat, feeling trapped.

But she realized she had to tell him. She had already made up her mind.

And he knew she was going to tell him. He didn't prod. He didn't say anything. Didn't look at her, either, as she sat trying to work up her courage, trying to decide where to start.

For that—for his patience—she was grateful.

"I grew up in California," she said finally, staring into the flames in the fireplace. "I was—well, I was pretty much a beach-bunny type, to be honest. I wanted to find a rich, handsome husband who would take care of me so I wouldn't have to work. I wanted to stay home and have babies and raise them."

She smiled faintly, remembering those long-ago dreams that seemed to have belonged to someone else—someone hopelessly young and naive.

"Thomas came along and basically swept me off my feet. He was so incredibly wonderful, in the beginning. I had no idea that he was an entirely different person inside from who he pretended to be."

She stole a look at Max.

He was nodding. "Like Julia," he said. "My wife had me fooled for a long time."

"Well, so did Thomas. He seemed to be everything I wanted, and he wanted me. I never could figure out why, until much later, after—after the marriage was over and he was . . ."

"Dead," Max supplied flatly.

"Yes." She cleared her throat. "He wanted me because I was passive, for one thing. And needy. I had lost my mother, and my father was remarried and already sick at that point. I was desperate for someone to hand me some kind of life."

"And he did."

"Yes. Thomas knew he was in charge of our relationship, that I would go along with anything he decided. And he knew that I had no interest in anything beyond being a wife and giving him children. I was impressed by his looks and his money, and who his parents were—"

"Who *were* they?"

"His father was—*is* Stephen Murdock, one of the most powerful lawyers in California. He handles a lot of high profile cases—celebrities, politicians, that type of thing. His name is always in the newspapers. And his mother, Marian, is from Texas. She's a DuPrix."

"A DuPrix? You mean the family that owns the big oil company in Houston?"

"That's the family. I expected them to be snobs about Thomas bringing home someone like me, but I was pleasantly surprised. Only later did I find out that everyone in their social circle knew about Thomas's temper. That he had abused several of his girlfriends. They never pressed charges—people like that would rather sweep problems under the rug than risk the publicity a police investigation would entail."

"That's disgusting."

"Yes, but it's the truth. Anyway, by the time I met Thomas, the suitable women he knew from the country club circuit were on to him."

"But you weren't."

"Of course not. I was oblivious. I lapped up every line he fed me. I think his parents were just relieved I didn't have any kind of baggage, anything that would make me a questionable candidate for a daughter-in-law."

"Meaning what?"

"Meaning, I had never been arrested, my parents weren't lowlifes. I wasn't even wrapped up in a career that would keep me from being a proper wife and mother. That was all I ever wanted to be."

"And Thomas gave you the chance."

"Exactly. When Thomas and I were married, we had the kind of wedding I had always dreamed of. It was like something out of a movie." She choked out a bitter laugh, remembering. "Hell, they released thousands of white butterflies at our ceremony and you should have seen the cake—layer upon layer, with the most elaborate frosting flowers you've ever seen."

"A fairy-tale wedding."

"Exactly." She shook her head. "I felt like a princess. I wore Marian's gown. It was made of yards and yards of silk and lace imported from Paris. And the way she treated me—it was almost like having a mother again. She called me the daughter she'd never had. That's part of why it hurt so much when . . ."

"When what?"

She chewed her lip. "When Thomas started beating me."

"I suspected as much," he said grimly.

"The first time was when I was pregnant. We were supposed to go to some charity dinner, and I told him I just couldn't make it. I had been nauseous for days—I had constant morning sickness—and I was exhausted. My father had died a few weeks before, and I was still grieving. Anyway, he gave me a black eye. Which meant that I couldn't go to any other dinners and parties until it healed, and that made him even more furious."

"But why?" Max asked, looking incredulous.

"Because I was supposed to be on his arm, playing the part of the corporate wife. I was supposed to be there to help him in social situations, because he wasn't very good at talking to people. He wanted me to smooth the way for him. He apologized, though, for what he had done that first time, and I believed him when he said it wouldn't happen again."

"But it did."

She nodded. "Not constantly, though. Not at first. It wasn't until after the baby came that it became regular."

"But why did you stay, Olivia?"

She shook her head. "Sometimes I don't know what I could possibly have been thinking."

He waited. That wasn't explanation enough.

"Other times," she said slowly, "I remember how it felt to be utterly alone in the world, without a plan or a goal, and then suddenly have this handsome husband and this respected extended family and a mansion in Pacific Palisades—and to be bringing a child into a world where he could have anything he would ever want or need, every privilege . . ."

She looked at him, saw his expression of disbelief.

"I know, Max. I know it doesn't make sense to you. Mostly, it doesn't make sense to me now, either. But I was so young and naive. I thought everything would be fine once we had the baby. And when it wasn't . . . I just wanted to keep him from hurting T.J."

"Did he?"

She closed her eyes briefly, not wanting to let the memory in. "I wanted Thomas to love his son," she said softly. "I even named him after his daddy. His real name is Thomas John. But Thomas was jealous of him from the moment he was born—jealous of the attention I gave him and the time it took to care for an infant. One day I caught him hitting the baby."

"Christ," Max muttered, his jaw clenched so hard she could see the muscles working in his neck.

"I was distraught. He said he was just disciplining him. That T.J. had almost broken a priceless piece of sculpture—a piece his mother had brought back from Paris years ago."

"So what? He was a child. It wasn't deliberate."

"That's what I told him. He said that I was way too lenient with him and that he needed a father's discipline. And you know what? I told myself that he was right."

"Oh, Olivia . . ."

"I told myself that maybe I *was* too indulgent. Maybe I *was* spoiling him. What was I thinking, Max?" she asked, a sob in her voice. "He was only a baby. You can't spoil a baby. You can't love a baby too much."

"No," Max said quietly. "You can't."

"I gradually started to notice bruises on T.J., especially one week when he was cutting his first tooth. One morning, after he had been up crying all night with teething pain, I caught Thomas hitting him again. I was horrified. This time, I left."

"Where did you go?"

"To the only place I could think of. My in-laws' home. They were always cordial to me. They showered the baby with presents when he was born, and even if they weren't the warmest grandparents in the world, they seemed proud of him. I thought that when I told them what had happened, they would want to help us. At least, help the baby. He was their own flesh and blood."

"But they didn't help you, did they?" Max asked.

"They accused me of overreacting. They called Thomas and told him where I was. He admitted maybe he'd gotten a little carried away because he'd been under so much stress since his father had made him a partner in the law firm. He vowed to learn how to control himself. I didn't want to take him back, Max, but he got to me when he said that his own father had been rough and overly stern with him and Gregory."

"His brother."

"Yes."

"What was he like?"

"Just like Thomas, really. Handsome. Smart. An attorney. He was also a partner in the family law firm, of course. He had a strong sense of honor and preserving the family name, just as Thomas and their parents did. They seemed to think that as long as everything appeared to the rest of the world to be fine, then it really was."

"That's twisted."

"I know. Meanwhile, eventually Thomas hit T.J. again. And this time, I had to rush him to the hospital. He was so tiny. His tiny little arms and chest were all black and blue . . ." She trailed off, unable to speak, paralyzed with emotion at the image she would never be able to erase from her mind.

"Oh, Olivia."

She was crying.

Max reached for her.

He held her, and she allowed the tears to flow, tears she had kept boxed up inside of her all these years.

Her cheek was against Max's broad chest, and she could feel his heart beating beneath his warm cotton sweater. She felt him stroking her hair, and she didn't want to push him away. This wasn't wrong. She needed him; needed his comfort; needed him to help her face the barrage of memories that surged up inside her as though a dam had broken.

"You don't have to tell me any more if you can't," Max said quietly after a while, still running his fingers across her hair in a rhythmic, soothing motion.

"No, I have to tell you. You deserve to know, and I-I've

never talked about it. In all these years, I've never told
another soul what happened."

"It's good for you to get it out then."

"Yes, and—I have to tell you." She straightened, looked
up at him. "Because he's found us, Max. As I told
you . . ."

"Gregory. Your brother-in-law."

"Yes. I'm afraid of him, Max. He blames me for
Thomas's death."

"What happened to Thomas?"

"When T.J. was hospitalized, I reported the incident to
the police. I had him arrested for child abuse. Gregory
and my mother- and father-in-law tried to talk me out of
it, of course. But I knew I had to do the right thing.
Thomas committed suicide in prison."

"The coward" was Max's biting reaction. "He couldn't
accept responsibility for his own actions."

"No. And his parents and brother were shattered. They
accused me of framing him. They said I wanted a divorce
and that I had seen this as my only way out without losing
custody of my son. They vowed to get custody after
Thomas died. Stephen had so many high-powered legal
contacts, and I had nothing. No money, no contacts, no
power to fight him in court."

"But you were his mother. And you said there were
other women Thomas had abused—"

"Yes, but Thomas was dead. I would be battling his
parents and Gregory, not him. Besides, those women
would never have come forward to help me. I told you,
they wanted the whole thing kept silent. That was how
Thomas got away with as much as he did his whole life.
Nobody wanted to talk. Nobody wanted to air the family's
dirty laundry."

"So, what happened?"

"They got a court order granting them visitation rights

and saying I couldn't leave town with my son until the case was settled."

"How did they manage that?"

"They had connections. I told you. Then Gregory came over one night—I was back in the house in the Palisades, though I knew it wouldn't be long before they managed to take that away from me. Anyway, Gregory told me that I might as well just hand T.J. over now. He called him Tommy," she added in a biting tone. "How I hated that name."

Max nodded.

She went on, "Gregory wanted me to just give in rather than dragging the whole family through a messy lawsuit. I told him he and his parents would never get my son away from me. He threatened me, and then he grew violent. He beat me even more viciously than Thomas ever had. He was a monster. And when he left that night, he told me that I'd better be careful, because a lot of people's lives—including T.J.'s—would be better if I were dead."

"He threatened to kill you?"

"Basically. I panicked. I took off the next day. Just packed up a few things and left town with T.J. Of course, they launched a massive search for us. For the first time in their lives, they used their family name to generate publicity. They staged a nationwide search for their 'kidnapped' grandson. I followed it from wherever I was. I lived in constant fear of being discovered, but nobody ever figured it out, as far as I know. Of course, I changed my appearance, and my name—"

"That's why," Max said, staring intently at her.

"That's why what?"

"You're not a natural brunette, are you?"

"No. I had blond hair. You could tell? Is it that obvious?"

"Something just didn't seem to mesh about you from the moment I met you. Even your name—"

"It's not Olivia."

"No," he said, shaking his head. "That doesn't suit you. What's your real name?"

"Katie," she said softly, and the sound of the old familiar name on her own lips was enough to bring tears to her eyes. "I was Katie. Katie Kenrick."

"Katie Kenrick?" He smiled, touched her cheek. "Yes, that's perfect. That's you."

"Not anymore. I'll never be who I was back then. I'll never get that part of me back. I'm always going to be running from them, Max."

"How can you be so sure? Why don't you just go to the police and tell them the truth? You're T.J.'s mother. He loves you. He belongs with you. You haven't done anything wrong."

"Then why did I run away? Can't you see how it would look to them, Max? To the police, and everyone else? The Murdocks have the influence and legal know-how to make it appear that I'm the bad guy in this situation. I'd never manage to win a custody battle with them, Max. And even though it's wrong to keep running, to bring T.J. up this way—I can't take a chance that they'll get their hands on him."

"But—"

"I should never have told you," she said, feeling a twinge of frantic anxiety welling up in her gut. "Max, you can't tell anyone. You can't turn me in—"

"Turn you in? I would never do that, Olivia. For God's sake, you can trust me. I thought you knew that. I'm on your side. I want to help you."

"Then help me escape," she said flatly. "Gregory knows where I am. He's probably on his way to Newberry Cove—if he's not here already. He wants me dead, Max. I've got to get out of here before he finds us. I can't leave any trace."

Max fixed his gaze on her, and there was no way of knowing what he was thinking.

Finally, he nodded. "You're right. You have to leave. There's no way around it. I just . . . I don't want to say goodbye, Olivia."

Surprised—and realizing, somewhere through the mist of fear and panic that had come over her, that she felt the same—she heard herself saying, "I don't want to say goodbye either."

"Maybe—"

"No." She put her fingers against his lips. "There's no way around it. We have to go. And we can't ever come back."

"But you're going to spend the rest of your life alone, always worrying and wondering and looking over your shoulder."

"I'll do anything I have to do to keep T.J. safe, Max."

"I know what you mean. I'd do the same thing, in your shoes. All right, Olivia. I'll help you get away."

"I want to leave the country. Can you get me to the Canadian border?"

He studied her. "You already have a plan?"

"I've been thinking about it. It makes the most sense. That's partly why I ended up here in Maine in the first place. I guess I was always thinking, in the back of my mind, that I could slip over the border if things got too risky."

"But if you go . . ."

"I know. If we go, we most likely won't ever come back."

"How will you survive on your own, Olivia? With no references, no friends or family, no job lined up—you can't even use your real identity. What are you going to do?"

"What I've done all along," she said wearily. "Start all over again. Get a job. A place to live."

"How do you get a job with no references?"

"You'd be surprised how easy it is, when you've got a child, to find somebody willing to pay you under the table and ask no questions. Dr. Klimek did it. He took one look at T.J. and he realized he wanted to help us."

"Never knew the old guy had it in him."

"He's a kind man," Olivia said. "He just doesn't know how to communicate, how to reach out to people. He's much better with animals."

"Shouldn't you tell him that you're going?"

She hesitated. "I don't know. I hate to just leave him like this. But I can't take any risks, Max. Gregory is after us. He's vicious."

"Maybe you're mistaken about him," Max said hopefully. "Maybe he isn't capable of—"

"Murder?" Olivia snorted. "I know him. He's ice, through and through, Max. He thinks I've brought dishonor to the family name. He holds me responsible for his brother's death. He wants me out of the picture so that he can get his hands on T.J.—the family's future. Thomas's legacy."

"Isn't Gregory married? Why doesn't he just have a kid of his own?"

"He can't," she said flatly. "Something about some drug he had to take when he was a kid—it left him sterile. He was married, a long time ago. When his wife found out, she divorced him. There was a time when I felt sorry for him. Now . . ." She shuddered. "Now I just want to be as far away as possible from him, Max. You have to help me."

"I'll help you, Olivia." He paused, then asked, with

obvious reluctance, as though he already anticipated her answer, "When do you want to go?"

"As soon as possible," she told him resolutely.

"Not tonight. It's getting late; T.J. is exhausted, and you can't scare him by taking him away in the middle of the night."

"No, not tonight," she agreed. "I know we're safe here, for the time being. But tomorrow . . ."

"Tomorrow? It's going to snow like crazy tomorrow, Olivia. Haven't you heard the forecast?"

"If you don't want to take a risk and come with me, I completely understand, Max. If the roads are bad—"

"My Explorer is fine in the snow. It's not that. I'll drive you. But are you sure it has to be that soon?"

She nodded, not meeting his gaze.

She didn't want to see anything in it that might tempt her to stay.

TEN

Max didn't make any pretenses about where he was going to sleep tonight.

While Olivia was soaking in the long, hot bath he had urged her to take, to relax her nerves, he put fresh flannel sheets on his bed and plumped the pillows.

He stashed the cans of paint and tools and buckets in the closet. He dusted his dresser top and bedside table with a sock from the laundry basket. Then he smoothed the ivory-and-red-patterned quilt on the bed—a quilt Sarah had given to him years ago.

To him and Julia, actually. She had made it by hand. As a wedding present.

Julia had hated it, of course. She'd grumbled that she couldn't believe that people in Newberry Cove thought it was acceptable, in this day and age, to give newlyweds actual wedding presents instead of cash. Didn't they know that these days, you just handed over an envelope to the bride and groom?

She had insisted that Max pack the quilt away. Why he had listened to her, he would never know.

Actually, he did know. It was because he had been young, smitten, and shamefully more interested in getting his new bride into bed than in what was covering it.

Alter Julia died, he came across the quilt and, despite

a pang of guilt, decided to use it. He found that it didn't remind him of Julia or their marriage; it reminded him of Sarah, and all she had done for him. She had been pleased to see it on his bed and didn't question its sudden reappearance. For that, he was grateful.

When Max had done all he could to make the room welcoming for Olivia, he stood back in the doorway and surveyed it.

It was pretty rough around the edges—spackled patches on the walls, moldings stripped away from the windows and doorway, unfinished wide plank floor.

But when he turned off the light and lit a vanilla-scented Yankee candle jar on the bedside table, the room looked cozy and inviting in the flickering candlelight.

Out the window, the snow was coming down now. Fat, lazy flakes swirled through the air and the wind rattled the panes. Max knew it was only a matter of time before the wind picked up significantly and more snow blew in on the cold front he'd heard about on the radio earlier. There were storm warnings posted through tomorrow afternoon.

Traveling up to the Canadian border wasn't going to be easy. Maybe he could convince Olivia to wait out the storm. But he didn't want to think about that now. He didn't want to think of anything beyond his plans for tonight.

He slipped quietly up the stairs to the loft, careful not to step on the familiar squeaky stair tread halfway up. There he saw the three children, all in sleeping bags on the floor between the beds. Lindsey was in her Little Mermaid sleeping bag; Sam's was the Rugrats, and T.J. was using the army-green one Max had bought for himself, with big plans of camping trips he and the twins were going to take last summer. They hadn't ever gotten around to it.

Maybe next year.

He found himself thinking that it would be fun if Olivia and T.J. came along with him, then caught himself.

They wouldn't be here.

They were leaving.

For good.

The knowledge left a hollow ache inside him, even though he knew it was for the best. If she stayed, he would want to give her things he couldn't possibly give to her, or to anyone. He would be tempted to forget the pain of the past and take another stab at a relationship—maybe even marriage.

Which, of course, was out of the question. He had learned the hard way that he was no competent judge of character, particularly when he was head over heels in—

Lust.

That, he told himself, was all he felt for Olivia.

Just as it was all he had felt for Julia.

He *wanted* Olivia.

Desperately, even.

So desperately that he was going to go downstairs and make passionate love to her all night long, if she'd let him.

Anything more was forbidden.

When she left, he'd have the memory of tonight to keep with him always.

He sighed softly and tucked Lindsey's exposed hand beneath the flap of her sleeping bag, then stooped to kiss her head. He did the same to Sam, smoothing his sweat-dampened blond hair from his forehead.

Then, pausing, he looked down at T.J.

The little boy looked so much like his mother. But his eyes lacked the perpetual wariness in Olivia's. He slept peacefully, tucked cozily between Max's children, unaware that tomorrow he would be uprooted once again, leaving behind everything that was familiar to him.

Max bent and smoothed T.J.'s hair just as tenderly as he had Sam's. Then, impulsively, he bent and placed a kiss on the little boy's cheek.

"I'm going to miss you, buddy," he whispered, feeling a lump threatening to rise in his throat.

He wondered what T.J.'s life would be like. Olivia was the most devoted mother Max had ever seen, but—a boy needed a dad. T.J. would never have a father.

Not unless Olivia met someone, someone she trusted. *The way she couldn't trust you,* Max told himself.

Abruptly, he rose and went downstairs.

Back in his room, he changed into a pair of red-and-blue flannel pajama bottoms and a gray thermal Henley shirt. He looked in the mirror, wondering if the combination matched, then deciding it didn't matter. With any luck, he wouldn't be wearing them for long.

He went to the back door, let Lady in, and bedded her down on the cushion where she always slept beside the kitchen stove. "Good dog," he whispered, patting her head. "Now go to sleep." He wanted no distractions.

He turned down the heat at the thermostat, double-checked to make sure all the doors and windows were locked, and closed the screen on the fireplace after stirring the dying embers.

Finally, there was nothing left to do but go back into the candle-lit bedroom, sit on the edge of the bed, and wait.

And wait.

Olivia was still in the tub twenty minutes later.

Finally, Max's impatience to have her in his bed got the best of him. Uncertain whether he was doing the right thing, but knowing he'd go crazy if he didn't take action, he went to the bathroom door and knocked softly.

"Olivia?" he whispered, even that sounding like a shout in the silent house.

There was no reply.

"Olivia?"

Fear slid like a clammy hand around his heart, and he paused with his hand on the knob, a dark, foreboding thought invading his mind.

What if Gregory Murdock had followed her here?

What if while Max was upstairs checking on the children, he had broken into the house, and—

Max jerked the knob and threw the door open, prepared to find the room empty and his worst fear confirmed.

But the room wasn't empty.

There she was.

Asleep in the tub, her head against the hard porcelain edge, resting there as peacefully as if it were a down pillow.

For a moment he could only stand there, staring at her naked body, feeling vaguely illicit in his voyeurism, yet unable to help himself.

She was incredible. Her breasts were full and softly rounded, her belly flat, her long arms and legs toned. Her skin was creamy white, except for a smattering of freckles above her breasts where the sun had kissed her long ago. Her lips were parted slightly in slumber, one hand tucked beneath her cheek, making her look like a child lost in dreamland.

He crossed the small room and picked up the towel she'd left on the floor beside the tub. He hesitated, knowing he had to wake her, wondering what she would do when she found him there and realized he'd been looking at her.

Well, so what? It wasn't as though they hadn't made

love. It wasn't as though he hadn't run his hands over every inch of that glorious body of hers.

Still, he'd never *seen* her. It had been dark in the bedroom that night. He had been too caught up in the need to touch, to feel; he hadn't taken the time to *look*.

He allowed himself to steal one more glimpse of her in the tub, telling himself he could carry the image with him after she left, hating that a memory was all he'd have left of her in a few more hours.

Then he bent and, holding the towel so that she could grab it from him if struck urgently by modesty, he gently touched her arm.

She stirred, licked her lips, and then slowly came awake as he watched in fascination, still standing over the tub.

Her eyes opened, fluttered, then flew wide open when she clearly realized that she had fallen asleep and she was naked and he was with her.

"Max?" she asked, sounding uncertain, looking dazed, but making no move to cover herself.

"You fell asleep."

She nodded. "I had a nightmare. At least, I thought it was a nightmare. But I just remembered that Gregory is—Oh, God, I—" She choked and bit her lip as though to keep it from trembling.

"It's okay." He stroked her arm, kneeling beside the tub.

"I'm sorry."

"Don't be sorry."

"You don't need this," she told him.

"I don't need what?"

"Me—" she said, and he wanted to protest instantly, with all his heart, *Yes, I do. Yes, I need you. Please, find a way to stay.*

But she had gone on. "—crashing into your life with all my problems, asking you to help me break the law—"

"You aren't breaking the law."

"I'm wanted on kidnapping charges."

"T.J. is your own son. You did what you had to do to save his life, and your own."

"You understand," she said softly, nodding. "I knew you would. No, I didn't know," she amended. "But I hoped. And—oh, I—I just realized we're sitting here having this entire conversation and I'm in the tub!"

She squirmed and started to sit up abruptly.

"It's okay," he said, dipping a hand into the water, testing it, fighting not to let his fingers drift up against her skin that was tantalizingly close.

"It's still hot," he commented. "You should stay in. I didn't mean to disturb you."

"No, I should get out."

He couldn't respond. He found himself unable to keep from letting his eyes slide from her face to her neck, to her breasts and her belly, and down . . .

Guiltily, he jerked his gaze up to meet hers again and saw that she was watching him. She knew exactly what he was doing, exactly what he was thinking.

"The water *is* still warm," she said quietly. She lifted a wet finger and trickled some drops across the back of his hand. "See?"

"Mmm." He was holding his breath, not daring to believe she might be suggesting the very thing he was yearning for.

"Why don't you come in?" she asked after a long moment, a coy smile playing at the edges of her mouth.

He grinned. "I thought you'd never ask."

He stood and undressed swiftly, conscious of her intent gaze on his body as he cast his clothes carelessly onto the newly tiled floor. He felt her eyes lingering on the part of him that wanted her most urgently. The knowledge that she could clearly see what she did to him made him throb more fervently with need.

He stepped into the tub and sank into the warm water beside her, reaching for her and pulling her to him. He groaned when he felt her naked, slippery flesh against him.

"All we have is tonight," she whispered, lightly running the backs of her fingers down his jaw.

He caught her hand and kissed it, then claimed her mouth.

She kissed him back feverishly, and he knew the raging hunger had consumed her as it had him. Her breasts were crushed against his chest, her legs entangled with his, her mouth open to his hot, probing tongue, and still he needed more, needed it right away.

He lowered his mouth to her breasts, turning his head from one to the other. She gasped as he teased her nipples to puckered peaks, writhing beneath him in an effort to position herself more intimately against him.

"Now, Max," she breathed hotly in his ear as he slid his mouth along the wet valley between her breasts and down along her flat belly.

"Now?" he protested, though he was ready, so ready he ached for her.

"I can't wait. Now," she urged, and he obliged swiftly.

He positioned her on his lap, facing him, and pulled her down, sinking fully into her. She whimpered in pleasure and wrapped her legs around his back as they rocked rhythmically, the water sloshing around them and lapping at the edges of the tub.

All too soon he realized he couldn't hold back and flung out her name as he exploded inside of her. When it was over he remained there, holding her, and they were as still as a lake after a boat's wake has subsided, simply staring at each other.

When he spoke, his voice was hoarse, unfamiliar to his own ears. "You should know—I've never felt like that before in my life, Olivia."

"I haven't either. I've never even come close."

They laughed softly, at nothing, really, and kissed— deep, long, languid kisses, taking their time now that the urgent need had been sated.

Finally, reluctantly, when the water grew tepid, they climbed out of the tub.

He handed her the towel and his robe that he'd laid out for her earlier, and wrapped a towel around his own waist, effectively concealing the growing evidence that he wanted her again.

"You're not sleeping on the couch," she said, almost playfully, as he opened the bathroom door and turned out the light.

"No," he agreed. "I'm not sleeping on the couch."

With that, he led her through the sleeping house to his candle-lit bedroom at last.

All too soon, they were seated across from each other at the kitchen table, the three children noisily discussing the merits of Cocoa Pebbles versus Cocoa Puffs—neither of which had been in Max's cupboard, to their dismay.

When the twins started arguing over who should get the last bit of Cap'n Crunch, he had pulled the box away from them and announced that there would be no cold cereal today.

He then busied himself making oatmeal—not the instant kind, either. The kind that came in the round cardboard box and had to be cooked on the stove.

Olivia had been positive T.J. wouldn't eat it. But when Max placed a bowl in front of him—with raisins for eyes,

nose, and a smiling mouth and a dusting of brown sugar
for hair—he dug right in.

Olivia couldn't stop looking at Max; she couldn't stop
thinking about how he'd made her feel in his bed last
night—all night.

She yawned. They hadn't slept; there had been no
time. Their moments together were ticking rapidly away;
she couldn't imagine wasting even one precious second
on sleep.

Now, seeing his hair pillow-tousled and the dark pin-
pricks of his morning beard shading his jaw, she was overwhelmed by a sense of comfort. She couldn't help but
feel as though she belonged here, with him, in this house.
And the children—

Every time she looked at her son, saw his smile, she
was slammed with the reality of all she was taking from
him.

Yet she had no choice.

She couldn't stay, even if she wanted to, even if Max
wanted her to—even if they decided to put aside their
differences and make a go of it together.

There was no decision to be made, no soul-searching
to do.

She was leaving, today.

It was over.

That was that.

But I care about him, she realized, watching him lift his
cobalt-blue coffee mug to his mouth with one hand while
steadying Lindsey's teetering glass of milk with the other.

If it weren't for Gregory . . .

What?

If it weren't for Gregory having found them, would she
stay? With him? Would they have a future?

No. Of course not. She would be a fool to remarry.
She couldn't expect anyone—and certainly not Max, who

had been through enough pain of his own—to share her furtive existence, to protect her secrets, to place himself, and his children, at risk. She wouldn't allow him to do that, even if he wanted to.

She stared as he set down his mug and bit into a piece of buttered toast, memorizing the cleft in his chin, the shade of his eyes.

It isn't fair, she thought desolately. *I want nothing more than to stay here with him and these children in this house, for the rest of my life. Why is that so much to ask?*

Such a simple dream.

And as out of reality's realm as if she had wished to be Queen of the World and live forever in a castle in the clouds.

"You okay?" he asked in a low voice, catching her wistful stare.

She nodded and dropped her gaze, toying with her napkin as though folding it into an accordion were the most fascinating challenge she had ever encountered.

As long as you have T.J. and you're far away from here, you'll be okay, she told herself firmly. *That's all that matters. Nothing else. Remember that.*

"I'll call Sarah as soon as we're done eating," he told her quietly, bending his head close to hers.

The children didn't notice, wrapped up in their own rollicking conversation.

"Sarah?" she echoed, not understanding.

"I'll ask her to come over and watch the kids. I can't bring them."

"No, you can't. But—"

"Don't worry. I won't tell her anything. And she won't ask."

"You read my mind."

"I'm getting pretty good at that," he said with a fleeting grin.

"I want to call Dr. Klimek, Max."

"Are you sure? I thought you didn't want to risk letting anyone know."

"I owe it to him. He gave me a job when I had no place else to turn. I don't want to leave him high and dry without warning, and I know I can trust him. After all, he wouldn't even tell *you* where I lived," she reminded him.

Max had told her about his effort to pry personal information about her from the old veterinarian the day he'd stopped at the office and left the note.

"Yes, I think you should call. I'm sure you can trust him," Max said, nodding. "You can go ahead and use the phone in the other room when you've finished eating. I'll keep the kids occupied. But what are you going to tell him?"

"No details. Just that I have to leave town suddenly. I mainly want to thank him for all he's done for me and T.J."

She swallowed hard over a sudden lump in her throat. T.J. considered the old man a friend, and so did she. Their only friend in Newberry Cove—until Max and his children had come along.

It figured that only now, when they were leaving, did this place seem to feel like home. Only now was there a compelling reason to stay.

"I'm going to make the call now," she said, pushing her chair back from the table.

She must have spoken more forcefully than she'd intended. Not only was Max watching her, but all three children had stopped talking and were looking at her with the same curious expression.

"Who do you have to call, Mom?" T.J. asked.

"Just . . . Dr. Klimek. It's about work. I'll be right back."

"Can I talk to him, too?" T.J. asked. "I want to find out how that little black kitten is doing—you know, the one whose paw got run over."

"I'll ask him about it," Olivia said, standing and glancing at Max.

He picked up her cue. "Hey, T.J., your oatmeal face is looking a little bald. Want me to add some more brown sugar to your bowl?"

"Sure!" T.J. said, breaking into a grin.

Olivia left the kitchen, marveling at Max's ability to zoom right in on the perfect distraction. T.J. never had been one to turn down anything sweet.

It had been so cute, the way Max had made those faces for the kids in their oatmeal. What other man would think of that charming extra touch? Certainly not Thomas.

The thought of her dead husband made the coffee and toast she'd consumed churn in Olivia's stomach.

Thomas.

Thank God he would never be able to bother her or T.J. ever again.

If only Gregory hadn't found them . . .

She scarcely dared to think of what would have happened if he hadn't.

They could have stayed in Newberry Cove. She might have eventually put aside her fear and allowed herself to fall in love with Max. He might have fallen in love with her. They might even have gotten married. She might have woken every morning for the rest of her life in his arms, might have been a mother to the twins, might have had more babies, with Max . . .

A lifetime with Max flashed before her eyes and she tried to blink away the tears, but they fell anyway.

She stood in the living room, listening to Max and T.J.

and the twins talking and laughing on the other side of the wall, and she mourned what could never be.

Gradually, as her tears subsided, the grief gave way to fury.

Damn Gregory Murdock!

Damn him for what he had stolen from her, and from T.J.

Hatred seethed through her, more powerful even than what she had felt toward Thomas for what he had done to her and T.J. Back then, she had foolishly thought they could put it behind them, heal, move on.

Now she knew she would never be able to forget or heal or move on. For the rest of her life.

She would have *no* life.

No freedom, no joy, no hope. She might as well be in prison.

That realization was so intensely devastating that, for a moment, she considered an option that had never crossed her mind until now.

What if she stayed . . . and fought?

What if she let Gregory Murdock confront her? What if she let him drag her to court?

No.

He might win.

He might take T.J. away from her. She couldn't possibly take that risk.

As long as she had her son, her life was worth living—on *any* terms.

Lifting her chin, she turned toward the telephone, knowing what she had to do. There was no use denying it, or trying to delay it, either. The sooner she and T.J. were on their way to Canada, the better.

She would just make this one call to Dr. Klimek, and then she would tell Max they had to get going.

She dialed the number of the clinic, knowing that was

where the veterinarian would be. So would she, at this hour on any other morning.

Sure enough, he picked up after a few rings.

"Dr. Klimek? This is Olivia."

"Olivia? Where are you?"

He had never been one to make warm chitchat, but his abrupt question and flat tone caught her off guard. So, he was angry that she wasn't there this morning.

Well, what did she expect?

She had a job to do. She wasn't doing it.

Her boss had every right to be provoked.

Knowing he wasn't going to like what she had to say, she pressed on, eager to get the phone call over with and almost wishing she hadn't called. "I'm just calling to tell you I'm leaving town, Dr. Klimek. Something has come up, and I'm afraid I have no choice."

There was a pause.

"Where are you going?" the doctor asked, his tone as detached as before.

"I'd rather not say. I just—thank you for all you've done for me and T.J."

There was no reply.

So, he was angry. He wasn't even going to wish her well.

"Where are you now? Are you at home?" he asked finally.

"No, I'm at Max Rothwell's house."

Only when the words had left her lips did she realize what she'd done. Why had she ever told him the truth? Why had she established any kind of link to Max?

Because she'd been so unnerved by the doctor's attitude—that was why. Because she hadn't wanted to leave on bad terms and because she trusted him.

Besides, Dr. Klimek never asked her any personal questions. The least she could do, now that he had, was answer it truthfully, since this particular information was pretty much harmless. He already knew Max was interested in her, so he wouldn't be surprised that she was with him now. Maybe he thought she had stopped by here to say goodbye to the Rothwells. In fact, if he asked, that was what she would say.

But he didn't ask.

All he said was a stiff, "All right, then."

Feeling awkward and wishing she had never called, Olivia softly said, "Goodbye. And thank you again."

There was a click on the other end of the line. He hadn't even wished her good luck or asked her to keep in touch.

Of course, she couldn't keep in touch.

But good luck, Olivia thought ruefully, she definitely could have used.

Trembling, Josef Klimek stared at the black-gloved hand that had broken the connection by pressing the button on the telephone.

"Very good, doctor," the man said mockingly. "I'm pleased. To be honest, I didn't think she was going to show up today—I didn't even think she'd call. But I'm glad I decided to wait around, just in case."

Dr. Klimek said nothing. He fought the urge to rub his temple where the butt of the man's gun had left a deep, bloody gash only moments before the phone had rung. His face was sticky where the blood had poured down from the wound.

His mind raced back over the events that had transpired ever since he had risen at dawn. After washing and dressing, he had fed the livestock and milked the cows, then made his solitary breakfast of eggs and sausage and toast.

He had eaten the same breakfast every day for the last fifty-odd years, since he had come to live on the ramshackle farm outside of town. But for the first decade, it had been hot and waiting on his plate when he came back from the barn. Beth would be there, waiting for him, pouring a steaming cup of coffee only when he had washed and taken his seat at the table.

Beth.

Never a morning went by that he didn't see her in the empty seat across from his in the old farmhouse kitchen. Or puttering by the stove. Or in the garden outside the window, where the roses she had planted as a young bride half a century ago still bloomed every June.

Never a morning when he didn't pause, after breakfast, to stare at her picture on the mantel in the living room. It had been taken the spring before she died, and in it, her eyes shone with a glorious secret, though her belly wasn't yet rounded with the baby who was, even then, growing inside her.

He'd lost them both—his wife and his unborn son—when a drunk driver plowed into Beth as she walked back from town with the mail one summer afternoon. Josef had died along with them, only nobody seemed to realize it.

They saw him going about his daily business, and they seemed to assume he had gone on with his life.

But Josef was only going through the motions. Getting up each morning, eating, working, sleeping—and all the while, he was merely waiting.

Waiting to see Beth again.

He knew the time wasn't far off now. He'd known it when he found the telltale lump on his neck several months ago. Finally, the wait was coming to an end.

Of course, he had done nothing about the lump. No reason to go to a doctor and get the diagnosis that he had already made himself. No reason to delay what was coming. Nothing to do but watch the lump grow—and quietly get his affairs in order, and rest whenever the incredible weariness overtook him.

It was getting harder and harder to get himself out of bed these days, but he did it, of course. Just as he had done it all these years without Beth.

And today was no different from any other day.

Until he had arrived at the clinic, everything was as it should have been.

Even then, he had seen Olivia's car in the parking lot and assumed she was inside. She usually arrived before he did to open the place.

But this morning, the building had been deserted.

Or so it had seemed.

Only when he had stepped into his office to hang his coat on the hook behind the door had he realized he wasn't alone. Out of the corner of his eye, he'd seen the shadow moving in the corner behind his desk. When he turned his head in that direction, he saw the stranger.

And the gun.

He had no idea who the man was or why he was so interested in Olivia's whereabouts. But clearly, telling the man anything about Olivia and T.J. might place them in danger. So Josef had kept quiet.

Even when the stranger had pistol-whipped him.

Even when the stranger had threatened to kill him if he didn't tell him where Olivia lived.

All Josef could think, through the blinding pain, was that he couldn't give in. No matter what. He had to protect Olivia and sweet little T.J. from this man with the hard, black eyes. He had to pray that they wouldn't show up, late, and walk right into the trap.

When the phone had rung, the stranger had forced

him to answer it. And when he had heard Olivia's voice, Josef's heart had sunk.

Please, Olivia, don't give anything away, he had begged silently, even as he asked the questions prompted by the stranger, who had cocked his gun and pressed it against Josef's temple as incentive.

Little did he know that Josef had been staring death in the face for months, welcoming it.

He wouldn't have asked her where she was if he had thought she'd answer. She never talked about herself, or her past. Just as Josef didn't talk about himself or his past. He figured that somewhere along the way, Olivia had faced the kind of pain he had when he'd lost Beth and his child. People who went through something like that couldn't be expected to talk about it.

So, he never asked her questions; and he had the feeling that even if he had, she wouldn't have answered them.

But today, for some reason, she did.

She said she was at Max Rothwell's house.

Why had she told him that?

If he had believed, for one instant, that she would reveal her whereabouts, he would have gladly let the stranger shoot that gun of his.

Max Rothwell's house.

What was she doing there?

Josef could only hope Max would keep her and T.J safe from this stranger if he showed up there. And he would, of course.

"Max Rothwell?" the stranger asked thoughtfully now that the connection was broken. "Who is he?"

"I—I don't know," Josef lied, despite the gun pressing against his temple.

"I'm sure you do." The man was well-spoken. Deadly calm. "She seemed to think you knew him, the w~~ said his name."

"She's wrong. I have no idea whom she's talking about," Josef said stoically.

"Rothwell . . . Rothwell . . ." The man lowered the gun but kept it trained on the doctor as he crossed over to the row of filing cabinets. Then he turned his back.

Josef helplessly watched him scanning the alphabetical labels on the drawers, knowing what was going to happen.

Sure enough, the man stopped at the one marked with the letter R and pulled it open. Frustrated when he kept fumbling, he pulled off his gloves and shoved them into his pockets, still clutching the gun. As he thumbed through the folders inside the drawer, Josef wondered what would happen if he tried to tackle the man while his back was turned.

There was no doubt what would happen.

He was old, and weak from the cancer that had ravaged his body.

The man was young and well-built and armed.

He frantically tried to think of a way to warn Olivia, even as the man pulled out a folder and turned to him.

"Rothwell, Max," he said, a gleam in his black eyes. "It appears that you're a bit forgetful in your old age, aren't you, doctor?"

Josef said nothing.

"Now I'll just have to hope that you keep thorough records and that I'll find this Max Rothwell's address inside of the folder, won't I? Well, what do you know? Here it is, right here."

"What do you want with Olivia?" Josef burst out, trepidation building as the stranger removed the information sheet from the file.

Amusement flickered in the stranger's gaze. "I might as well tell you, old man. She's wanted by the authorities."

"Wanted? For what?" Josef asked, certain the man was ~~ng.~~

He had sensed from the moment Olivia showed up at his clinic several years ago that she was a good person to whom something terrible had happened. That was why he'd hired her without references, no questions asked.

He had learned long ago to trust his instincts.

"She's wanted for kidnapping, actually."

"Kidnapping!" Josef echoed in disbelief "What are you talking about?"

"It's true. She kidnaped the little boy."

T.J.? Josef was incredulous. The child obviously belonged to her; they looked too much alike. And the child obviously adored her. She was a wonderful mother. There was no way she had done anything to harm the boy, or ever would.

The man was lying. He had to be.

Or if Olivia really had kidnapped the little boy, she'd had good reason.

Josef looked the stranger in the eye, his body rigid with anger. "Leave Olivia alone," he said gruffly.

"I'll be glad to. After we settle our little legal problem," the man said, putting his gloves back on and carefully wiping the handle of the gun. Not wanting to leave prints, Josef realized with a chill.

"I do thank you for your help, Dr. Klimek," the man announced with the air of someone who was in a hurry to get going.

Josef frowned. So, this was it? The stranger was going to leave? Didn't he realize that the moment he walked out the door, Josef would call Max's house to warn Olivia?

Of course he realized it.

Josef saw that the gun was once again raised and cocked, aimed right at him.

So, this was how it was going to end. Not peacefully in his bed, after all.

Surprise and regret mingled in Josef's mind as he closed his eyes and braced himself for the inevitable.

He heard the gun go off.

His first thought was that he felt no pain where the bullet slammed into his body . . .

His next thought was that he'd been wrong, that it hurt like hell, that the pain was too much to bear . . .

His last thought was of Beth.

And Josef died with a faint smile on his lips.

ELEVEN

"What did he say?" Max asked, slipping into the living room and finding Olivia beside the phone, a faraway expression on her face.

She turned to him. "Where are the kids?" she asked.

"Outside, throwing out seed for the birds. What did he say?" he repeated.

"Dr. Klimek? Let's just say he wasn't happy that I'm leaving."

Nobody is, Max thought grimly. Aloud, he asked, "Did he give you a hard time?"

"A hard time? Not really. He isn't the type. But I feel bad. He's a nice old man, and I know T.J. is going to miss him."

"He'll forget, eventually."

"Do you really think so?"

Max shrugged, aching inside for the little boy whose life was going to change so drastically without warning. "I think T.J. is going to be just fine, he said, needing to reassure her, needing to wipe the pain from her face. "After all, little kids usually bounce back fairly quickly."

"What about me? Am I going to bounce back?"

"I'm sure you will, eventually," he managed.

"You're wrong." Olivia wrapped her arms around herself, hugging her middle. Sensing that she would lose her composure if he touched her, he fought the urge to take her into his own embrace. "I'm not going to bounce back."

"You have before. You've started over before. Twice."

"But that was different."

"How?"

"I wasn't leaving you," she said, so softly that, at first, he wasn't sure he'd heard her right. But when she raised her eyes to his and he saw the expression in them, he knew.

"Maybe you don't have to, Olivia," he heard himself say. "At least, not yet."

"You mean, because it's snowing? I'm sure the roads are all right."

"That's not what I meant. I meant—"

"No, don't even go there, Max. I already thought about staying. I tried to figure out a way. And I can't. There's no way I can take a chance with T.J. I'd never win a custody battle. We've already been over this."

"No, I know that. It's not what I'm saying."

"What are you saying?" she asked breathlessly, and he could feel her anticipation, her fervent hope that he'd come up with a way for them to stay together.

"I'm coming with you. Me and the kids. We'll all go."

"No."

"Yes." He reached for her. "Olivia, listen to me—"

"No!" She pulled away from his grasp. "Max, you listen to me. You can't come."

"Why not? I have no ties to this place—"

"Of course you have ties. It's your home. The only place that's ever been home to you."

"I moved myself out of the town because I didn't feel connected anymore. Remember what I told you? I don't want to be here."

"It's home for Sam and Lindsey."

"Only because it's the only thing they know. They would be happy anywhere, as long as I was with them—and with you, and T.J., too, they'd have everything they need, Olivia."

"They wouldn't have roots."

"Who says? We'd find a place where we could have roots. We'd settle in some small town someplace, Olivia, and it would become home. We'd build a cabin, just like this one—"

"And someday, when Gregory finds me again, we'd flee it in the middle of the night. With the kids. We'd find a new town and try to make a new home, and Gregory would find us again." She was sobbing as she spoke, quietly, conscious that the children could come in and overhear at any moment.

He, too, kept this voice low. "He might not find us again, Olivia. Not if we left the country."

"But he might. No matter where I go, Max, I'm always going to be looking over my shoulder. I'm never going to have a moment's peace. I can't ask you to share that kind of life."

"You didn't ask."

"Well, then, I can't allow you to share it."

"I want to, Olivia. I want to take care of you, and T.J."

"But you have two children of your own to take care of, Max. Sam and Lindsey come first. You can't force this kind of life on them. If it were just you, then—"

"Then you'd want me to come?" he asked when she broke off.

She didn't reply.

"Olivia?"

"I don't know," she said in a voice that was barely audible. "I promised myself I would never let another man—"

"Hurt you? I wouldn't. You know that. You have to know that."

"You wouldn't intentionally. But how could I ask you to give up everything for me—your home, your freedom, your safety—and expect you not to resent it somewhere along the way?"

"I would never resent it," he insisted, although somewhere deep inside him, there was a flicker of doubt.

He had already made the mistake of falling for a woman who had expected—no, demanded—that he give up everything for her. He had resented the hell out of her.

Olivia isn't Julia, he reminded himself, as he had too many times in these past few weeks.

But would that matter in the end? If he found himself living his life on somebody else's terms—anybody else's terms—would he really be happy?

"Even if you didn't resent it," Olivia was saying, "that's beside the point. Because you have two children, Max. And you need to put their needs first."

The children.

Sam and Lindsey.

Yes, he had to put their needs first.

Their mother never had.

It was up to him to do what was right for them. He was all they had left.

"You're right," he told Olivia, nodding. "Sam and Lindsey come first. I can't make them live that kind of life."

He saw the fleeting disappointment in her eyes, knew that she'd been holding out one last hope, however slim, that he might talk her—and himself—into it. That he might insist on coming with her.

He hated the stark loneliness he saw in her gaze now, but there was nothing he could do to change it. They both knew she had to go.

"So, I'll call Sarah," he said.

She nodded.

He called.

Even as he dialed and listened to the phone ringing, he found himself wanting to delay their parting, if only for another few hours. He prayed that Sarah wouldn't be home or that she'd be unwilling to come and watch the twins, maybe overnight.

But of course she was home and of course she told him she'd be over in an hour, as soon as she'd taken her pecan sticky rolls out of the oven.

He hung up and looked at Olivia. "So, that's it, then. She'll be here soon."

"Good. You won't tell her or Sam and Lindsey where we're going?"

"You know I won't."

"Thanks, Max. I wish I didn't have to involve you."

"You don't have a choice, Olivia. I'll help you get away. It's the only way I'll know for sure that you're safe."

She nodded.

He stared at her, memorizing her face, longing for one last glimpse of the playful, joyous Olivia he'd seen last night.

"Oh, Max," she whispered, tears glistening in her eyes. "I wish things could have been different."

"So do I."

He leaned down and touched his forehead to hers, and they stood there for a long time, lost in thought.

Then Max gently slipped a finger beneath her chin and tipped her face up to his. He captured her lips tenderly beneath his, in a soft, sweet kiss that left him trembling.

She looked up at him desolately when it was over.

He was afraid to speak, knowing his voice would break, knowing he would beg her to do the impossible . . .

To stay.

To make it work, somehow.

To take a chance.

But they couldn't make it work and she couldn't take a chance. He wouldn't allow her to take a chance. Not with her child. Not with her life.

The silence was broken by the sound of a creaking door, childish chatter, and several pairs of small boots stamping snow in the mud room.

He turned away from Olivia, told her resolutely, "I'm going to go take a shower and get dressed. Maybe you can put on a video for the kids to watch upstairs while we wait for Sarah."

She didn't argue.

He left the room filled with a hollow ache and knowing he might as well get used to it.

Olivia paced Max's bedroom, listening to the faint sound of the pipes creaking as the shower started running in the bathroom.

She was physically ill at the thought of leaving him.

Here in this house, she felt, for the first time since childhood, as though she were home.

Home in the sense of belonging, as she had years ago when her parents were alive and she was Katie, carefree Katie, blissful and oblivious to the rough road ahead.

In this log cabin, tucked away in the Maine woods, she had found something she had thought she had lost forever.

Now she would lose it again.

Her mind raced over the conversation they'd just had out in the living room. He had offered to come with her.

Why hadn't she let him?

After all, they were leaving the country. There was a good chance Gregory might never find them in Canada.

Why couldn't she be optimistic?

Why couldn't she throw caution to the wind and just stay here, with him? Let Gregory confront her, let him try to take T.J. away from her. She was T.J.'s mother, for God's sake. Gregory had a history of abuse, just as his brother had. No court in its right mind would award custody to the Murdocks, given the circumstances.

But again came the harsh reality.

The Murdocks had a couple of things Olivia didn't have.

Money.

Power.

Olivia was the one who had run away—run for her life, and T.J.'s; but what if the judge didn't believe that? What if Gregory and his parents convinced him that she was just a delusional, bitter widow determined to keep the Murdock heir away from his late father's family? Who could come to her defense?

Her parents were dead.

Her stepmother was a virtual stranger.

And she'd cut herself off from all her old friends when she'd married Thomas. That had been his doing, she now realized. His way of forcing her to depend only on him; his way of being the only thing in her life.

Until T.J. came along.

T.J., her precious son.

She had lived only for him from the moment he was born.

She had vowed to protect him, and she would.

At any cost.

How could she have wavered from that promise, even for an instant?

Max.

When he was around, she found it impossible to stay focused.

She found herself considering things she had no business even thinking about.

When Max was around, she found herself tempted to trade her son, her baby, for a man she barely knew, when it came right down to it.

Shaken at the realization that her lust for Max was that potent, that dangerous, Olivia looked at herself in the mirror.

Who are you? she asked the woman she saw reflected there.

You don't look like me.

You want to do things that I swore I would never do.

You want to give up the most precious thing in your life for something that's only an illusion.

Hadn't she known all along that Max could never love her?

Hadn't he come right out and told her that himself?

"I have to get out of here," Olivia told the woman in the mirror. "Now. Without him."

If she spent even another moment with Max, there was no telling what she might do.

She had been right all along. She couldn't trust anyone.

Not even herself.

Max stepped out of the shower and reached for a towel, feeling for it on the edge of the sink that was barely visible in the steamy bathroom.

He really had to get around to installing the fan in the ceiling. Just one more in a long list of projects that had all but consumed him until Olivia came along.

Well, now she was leaving.

Things would be back to normal.

He could devote himself to his house and his children, the way he should have all along.

He was still reeling from the knowledge that he had almost considered dragging Sam and Lindsey up to Canada just so that he could satisfy his lust for a woman whose baggage made Julia look positively low-maintenance.

Now, without Olivia standing in front of him, so vulnerable and so beautiful, he could finally think straight.

Of course there was no way he could follow her to Canada.

Thank goodness she hadn't agreed to his ridiculous offer.

The sooner he got her out of his life, the better.

He wiped at the foggy mirror with a towel, then took his time shaving at the sink, not wanting to see her again until he absolutely had to. He could hear the faint sound of the children's video coming from the loft above.

Mary Poppins.

Julie Andrews was singing in that lilting voice of hers, and Max found himself irritated by her upbeat lyrics about a spoonful of sugar. It reminded him of T.J. and the oatmeal and how his little face had lit up when Max spooned extra brown sugar around the rim of the bowl to make more hair for the raisin face.

"I never knew oatmeal was so delicious!" he had exclaimed, taking another big mouthful after his mother had gone into the next room to make her phone call.

"Everything Daddy makes is delicious," Lindsey had said.

"Except beets," Sam had told her.

"Right. Except beets."

"I've never had beets," T.J. responded.

"That's because you don't have a daddy who makes them for you," Lindsey announced. "If you want, we can share our daddy with you. Right, Daddy?"

T.J.'s hopeful expression when he turned to look at Max had filled Max with a peculiar mixture of pleasure and pain.

He wanted T.J. to like him. Maybe even love him.

But the little boy would never be his son. He would never see T.J. again.

In that moment, Max had realized how much he was going to miss him. Just as he'd miss Olivia.

But since there was no way around it, the sooner they were out of his life, the better.

He set his razor carefully on the edge of the sink and took a last look in the mirror. He had missed a few spots shaving, but didn't bother to go back and clear the remaining stubble. Why bother? He looked like hell. His skin was pale, and his eyes were underscored by deep purple trenches, testimony to the sleepless night. Suddenly he felt sore and impossibly weary right to his very bones.

How heavenly it would be to climb into bed, wrap himself in Sarah's big quilt, and lose himself in a deep, dreamless sleep.

He smirked at his reflection.

That wasn't going to happen.

Not anytime soon.

He had a big trip ahead of him, and he had a feeling that when he returned his solitary nights were going to be anything but restful.

Sighing, Max pulled on his robe—the one he'd lent to Olivia. The herbal scent of her skin wailed from the thick folds of fabric. It seemed like a lifetime ago that he had sat across the breakfast table from her as she wore this robe.

And it would never happen again.

Max opened the door, struck by the chill of the rest of the house once he left the steamy bathroom. It felt empty already.

The bedroom was vacant.

Just as well.

Olivia must be upstairs with the kids.

What had she told T.J., if anything, about where they were going?

Max figured she was going to let her son think Max was driving them home. But Sam and Lindsey . . .

And Sarah . . .

He'd have to think of something to tell them. Especially since he wouldn't be back for quite a while.

The trouble was, he couldn't think of a reasonable lie.

Nor could he consider telling the truth.

Damn her for getting me into this mess, he thought. *Damn her for looking at me with those big, scared eyes of hers and making me think it's my duty to watch out for her. If I were smart, I would have turned my back and walked away the minute I realized she had something to hide.*

But he hadn't done that, and now it was too late. He was stuck. And he would follow through . . . for T.J.'s sake.

If he just kept in mind that he was doing all this to help a fatherless little boy, he would be all right.

Max dressed quickly, pulling on thermal underwear beneath his jeans and an extra tee shirt under layers of flannel and fleece. It was snowing in earnest now, and he wondered briefly if they should delay the trip until the weather cleared.

But that would mean spending another night in this house with Olivia. And though one of them could sleep on the couch, he had a feeling neither of them would—regardless of his renewed anger toward her. He might resent her for turning his life upside down; he might want her out of it as soon as possible, but when it came right down to it, he couldn't seem to resist the woman. Nor did he want to try.

No, he had to get her and T.J. out of here today.

Belatedly, he remembered that there was another reason they should leave quickly—a reason far more pressing than his own selfish emotional needs.

Gregory Murdock knew where Olivia was. He was coming after her.

From what Olivia had told Max about her brother-in-law, she had every reason to fear him.

Max bristled at the thought of anyone trying to harm Olivia. Just let him try it while Max was around.

He paused, dressed, standing in the middle of his bedroom.

Then he closed the door firmly after peering out into the living room to make sure Olivia and the children weren't nearby. He walked slowly to the closet and felt around on the inside wall for a nail high above the door frame. On it was a key he rarely took down, but he did so now.

Then, stretching above his head, he moved a stack of sweaters from the closet shelf. Behind them was a gray metal box.

He took the box and the key over to his bed, opened the lock, and lifted the lid.

There wasn't much inside.

Just a few important documents—the children's birth certificates and social security cards, his own passport, which he'd never used. Julia had insisted he get one when she was dreaming of a European honeymoon. Instead, they'd gone to Cape Cod. Julia had spent the entire week grumbling that they should be in Paris.

That had been his first inkling that his marriage wouldn't be entirely blissful. He should have gotten out right then and there—left his pouty bride in the quaint old Chatham bed-and-breakfast she had so eloquently deemed "a hellhole."

But if he'd left then, he wouldn't have the twins. The

years of heartache with Julia were more than worthwhile when he thought about his children.

Also in the metal box were the diamond engagement ring and wedding band he'd given Julia. She'd stopped wearing the engagement ring when they'd gotten married, saying it was too small and she'd wait until the day when he could afford "a real ring."

As for the platinum wedding band encrusted with diamonds—well, he'd splurged on that. He'd still been paying it off after she died. But she'd picked it out, and he couldn't bear to tell her it was too expensive. She'd been so proud to wear it at first, getting manicures several times a week so that her nails would be impeccable when she showed it off.

But she'd taken it off while she was pregnant with the twins. Her fingers had become so swollen she feared they'd have to saw it off. And after she had the babies . . . well, she hadn't bothered to put the ring back on. By then, their marriage was over anyway.

Max picked up the rings and turned them over in his hands, wondering if he should just sell them and get it over with. He'd thought he should keep them for Lindsey; that she might want them someday. But she didn't know what her parents' marriage had really been like. If she ever found out, would she want the rings?

Better let her decide, Max thought, tossing the rings back into the box, where they made a dull clanking sound when they hit the metal surface.

He reached back in and retrieved the one other item inside the box.

The small handgun had belonged to his father. Jack had always kept a gun in the house, though there was no crime to speak of in Newberry Cove. And when he died, Julia insisted that Max take it. She said she felt better knowing she could defend herself if anyone ever broke in.

After *she* died, Max had had every intention of getting rid of the thing. He couldn't bear the thought of the children getting hold of it. But Andy had pointed out that if he were going to live out here in the middle of nowhere, he should probably keep it around, just in case.

So he had.

But he had hidden it where the kids would never look and had locked it away as an added precaution. He also stored the bullets separately. They were in the top drawer of his dresser. He retrieved them now, tucking them into one zippered inside pocket of his parka and the gun into the other.

He was ready.

Let Gregory Murdock try anything while Max was around. He would defend Olivia and T.J at any cost.

He stepped out of the bedroom and stood still, listening.

Upstairs, Dick Van Dyke, as Burt the chimney sweep, was singing in his cockney accent.

Outside, he could hear the distant crunch of tires on the snowy driveway.

He glanced out the window.

Sure enough, there was Sarah's white Buick on its way up to the house.

But . . .

Max frowned, realizing there were already tire marks in the snowy driveway, ahead of Sarah's car.

What—?

Trying to ignore a stab of fear in his gut, he moved quickly to the bottom of the steps.

"Sam?" he called. "Lindsey?"

"Yes, Daddy?" came the instant reply.

Relief shot through him.

"Olivia?" he asked.

No answer.

"Olivia?" he called louder. "T.J.?"

Sam appeared at the top of the steps.

"Oh, they left, Daddy."

"They *left*?"

Sam nodded blandly. "Olivia said to tell you she had to borrow your truck to run an errand. She made T.J. go with her. He was real mad."

"He never saw *Mary Poppins* before," Lindsey added, popping into sight next to Sam. "He wanted to see the rest of it, but Olivia said they had to go *right now.*"

"How long ago was that?" Max asked, his heart pounding.

He should have known she wouldn't wait for him. He had wasted all this time getting ready, thinking she was right upstairs, when all the while she had set out without him.

Now she and T.J. were out there alone, with some nut after them.

"Dammit, Olivia," he said under his breath.

"What, Daddy?"

"Nothing," he muttered, glancing out the window again.

It was snowing like crazy.

He heard Sarah's car engine turn off.

"Listen, Sam, Lindsey," he said, pulling on his parka and feeling for the telltale lumps in the zippered pockets for reassurance. "I have to go out for a while."

"But Olivia took your truck," Sam said matter-of-factly.

"I know. I'll borrow Sarah's car. I'll be back later—"

"When later?"

"Just . . . I'm not sure. Be good for Sarah, okay?"

"What about Olivia and T.J.?" Lindsey asked, one eye on the television screen behind her.

"What about them?"

"What should we tell them when they come back? Olivia will probably want to see you. I think she really likes you, Daddy."

"Yeah, and T.J. wants her to marry you so that you can be his daddy, too," Sam said. "Then he would be our brother."

Max fought the urge to snap his reply. "Olivia and I aren't getting married," he told the twins, striving for patience.

"Why not?" Lindsey wanted to know.

"She would be such a good mommy," Sam said.

"Yeah, she's an angel. I'd love to have an angel for a mommy."

"Lindsey," Max said, then paused helplessly.

Sarah's footsteps sounded on the porch.

"Listen, I have to go," he told the twins. "When I get home, we'll talk about why Olivia and I can't get married. Okay?"

He turned his back on their disappointed faces, pulling on his shearling gloves and striding toward the door.

One step at a time, he told himself, taking a deep breath. First he had to find Olivia and T.J. and see them safely across the Canadian border.

Then he'd worry about breaking his children's hearts by telling them that not only would Olivia never be their mother and T.J. never be their brother, but that they would never be coming back here again.

Olivia strained to see out the windshield of the Explorer.

The wipers were working furiously to clear the driving snow, but visibility was poor and it was all she could do to keep the vehicle on the narrow, winding road through the woods. She'd passed another car a mile back, noting that it turned into Max's driveway just after it passed her.

Sarah? Of course.

By now, Max must have figured out that she had taken T.J.—and his car—and made a run for it.

I'm sorry, Max, she told him silently, her hands gripping the wheel.

She planned to leave the Explorer parked someplace at the first opportunity and mail the key back to him, along with instructions on where to find it. She couldn't do it in Newberry Cove, but she wouldn't go far.

Then she'd rent a car and continue toward the border with T.J. If this storm kept up, they might have to stop someplace and wait it out; but she wasn't worried about that. As long as they were a safe distance away from Newberry Cove, they'd be okay for a little while at least.

Even if Gregory tried to pick up their trail at that point, he wouldn't come up with much.

Olivia sighed and glanced at T.J. beside her. He was scowling, looking straight ahead out the windshield, his hands folded across his chest. He'd been that way ever since they'd left Max's house.

"Is your seat belt on nice and tight, T.J.?" Olivia asked conversationally.

He nodded, still scowling.

"I'm sorry I couldn't let you watch the rest of your video. I'll tell you what. I'll buy it for you and then you can see the rest of it, okay?"

"Why do you have to buy it for me?"

"Don't you want it?"

"Why can't I just watch it at Lindsey and Sam's house next time we go over?" he asked. There was a hint of suspicion in his voice.

Her heart sank.

"Maybe you can," she lied, because it was easier than

telling him any part of the truth. She couldn't do that.
Not yet.

"I don't see what the big rush was. Why did we have
to leave so fast? I didn't even get to say goodbye to Max
or thank him for the oatmeal."

"I know. I'm sorry. I was just . . . in a hurry."

"But why?"

"Because . . . we have to be someplace."

"Where?"

"I can't tell you, T.J.," she said reluctantly. "Just . . .
trust me, okay? Do you trust me? Can you just do what
I tell you to do from here on in without asking questions?"

"Why can't I ask questions?"

"T.J., come on. Please . . . it's hard enough to drive in
this weather without—"

She broke off abruptly, staring ahead into the swirling
snow.

"What's the matter?" T.J. asked promptly.

"Nothing," she murmured.

So a pair of headlights was approaching.

So what?

That didn't mean anything.

But she couldn't seem to shake the sudden, nagging
feeling of dread that settled over her like a dark hood.
She squinted through the windshield, watching the car
approach.

No, it wasn't a car.

It was a truck.

Dr. Klimek's truck, she realized as it started to pass her
on the narrow road.

Startled, she hit the brakes. The Explorer went into a
slide, spinning off the road.

Olivia shrieked and steered into the skid, fighting the

urge to slam on the brakes again, knowing that would only make things worse.

"Hang on, T.J.!" she yelled as they careened madly toward a clump of trees.

Images flashed before her eyes.

T.J. as a baby, snuggled safe in her arms . . .

Gregory's sneering face . . .

The rundown farmhouse in Newberry Cove . . .

Sam and Lindsey, floundering in the gray, choppy water . . .

Max.

His name whirled frantically from her lips as she reached for T.J. and ducked her head, knowing they were going to crash.

But the Explorer missed the clump of trees and the next thing Olivia knew, they had spun around once more and come to a stop in deep snow at the side of the road.

For a moment, there was only silence.

Then T.J. sobbed and Olivia unbuckled his seat belt, pulling him into her arms.

"It's okay, sweetheart," she crooned, stroking his hair. "It's all right."

"I thought—"

"I know; so did I," she said, her heart still raging against her ribs. She looked out at the snow-covered landscape, wondering how they were going to get out of here. It would be impossible, without help.

Grimly, she realized that they would have no choice but to trudge the mile or two back to Max's house. She knew he'd be angry that she had left without him—without even saying goodbye. He might be angry, too, that she had taken his truck without asking.

Well, she'd have to face him.

And Dr. Klimek, too. The old man had obviously been

on his way to Max's house. Why? What reason could he have for wanting to see her before she left?

Maybe he just wanted to say goodbye to T.J., Olivia reasoned.

"Listen, T.J.," she said, "We're going to have to walk back for help. I want you to make sure your coat is all zipped up and—"

"We don't have to do that, Mom," he interrupted, pointing out the rear window. "Look, there's Dr. Klimek. He can help us."

She turned to see that the veterinarian's old truck had pulled up on the road nearby. He must have seen what had happened to them after he passed and turned around to come back and help out.

Thankful to be spared the long walk through the snow with T.J., she zipped her own coat and opened the door.

"Stay here," she told T.J., who was still in his seat. "I don't want you to get cold and wet."

"What are you going to do?"

"I don't know," she admitted, doubting that the frail old man could help her push the snow-mired Explorer back onto the road.

But at least he could give them a ride back to Max's.

Which meant she'd still have to face him.

Setting her jaw, she stepped out into the frigid cold. Instantly, granular snow hit her exposed face, stinging her cheeks and chin. She ducked her head and started to wade toward the doctor's truck on the road.

It was still running.

She saw that he was getting out on the driver's side.

"Hello, Dr. Klimek," she called as the bundled figure came around the front of the truck, heading toward her.

He didn't reply.

Either he hadn't heard her or—

She froze.

The man walking toward her wasn't Dr. Klimek.

He was too short, too bulky, too young.

A truth more chilling than the wind-driven snow crept over Olivia.

The man driving Dr. Klimek's truck . . .

The man who was now just a few feet away, reaching into the pocket of his coat . . .

. . . was Gregory Murdock.

Before Olivia could move, speak, or run, a gun was leveled at her.

"Don't even think about trying to get away," Gregory Murdock warned her. "If you so much as move a muscle, believe me, I'll kill you."

TWELVE

Max cursed as the old white Buick went into yet another skid at the end of the long drive leading from his house to the winding woodland road.

Sarah shouldn't be driving around in weather like this on tires like these. If he had his Explorer, he would have no problem making his way out of here. But as it was, he'd be lucky to even get to the highway five miles down the road, let alone catch up to Olivia and T.J.

Sarah said she had passed them just before she pulled into his drive, which meant they were probably a few miles away now, even in the snow. The Explorer had four-wheel drive, and Olivia would be in a hurry to get away.

Worry mingled with his anger as Max thought of her and T.J. out in this storm alone. The woman was a damned fool—

No, he corrected himself, softening.

Olivia wasn't a fool. She was being hunted by her worst enemy, a man who meant to harm her—and take away her child.

He couldn't fault her for leaving when she had, the way she had.

If only she had waited for him, though. If only she had believed that he would take care of her, that he would see her safely to the border and then say goodbye.

Had she left him behind because she didn't trust him—
or because she didn't trust herself?

He might never know, he realized, steering carefully
back to the center of the drive and then making the turn
onto the rutted, unplowed dirt road.

He crept along in the tire tracks the Explorer had left,
noting with dismay that the snow had almost blown over
them. He would never catch up to her. Never.

But he had to try.

Olivia was motionless, staring at Gregory Murdock as
he advanced, the gun aimed squarely at her chest.

Her thoughts reeled.

How had he gotten Dr. Klimek's truck?

He must have gone to the clinic. That was how he knew
where to find her. Had the old man told him where she
was?

Olivia couldn't believe that. Even if Dr. Klimek were
angry with her for leaving without notice, he wouldn't
betray her whereabouts to a man like Gregory Murdock.

Then again, Dr. Klimek might not realize she was in
danger. Gregory was a master of deception. He could
come across as congenial, even well-meaning. He might
have convinced the doctor that he was a friend—or even
told him the truth: that he was T.J.'s long lost uncle and
that Olivia had kidnapped her own son and had been on
the run for several years.

All he would have to do was pull out a newspaper clipping or one of those "Missing Child" fliers as proof.

But . . .

If Gregory had persuaded Dr. Klimek to tell him where
Olivia was and if Dr. Klimek believed the worst about
her . . .

Why was Gregory driving his truck?

And where was the old veterinarian?

Olivia fought back a finger of fear. *Stay calm,* she told herself. *Don't think about anything but how you're going to get out of this alive and keep Gregory away from T.J. Maybe he doesn't know he's in the truck . . .*

"Where's the kid?"

Murdock's question seemed to echo her thoughts, and she warned herself to give nothing away before she answered, "Home."

"Home, where?"

She shrugged.

So, he didn't know T.J. was with her. He must not have been able to see his head in the passenger's seat when he passed.

"I asked you, where?"

"Do you really think I'm going to tell you, Gregory?"

"Do you really think I'm going to let you get away with not telling me, Kate?"

"You bastard," she muttered through gritted teeth, fury flaring at the sound of her old name on his lips—the name she had been forced to give up because of him. "I'll never tell you anything."

He cocked the gun. "Have it your way, Katie. I'll find him."

"No, you won't."

"Really?" He laughed. "I found you."

Keep him talking, she told herself. *If you keep him talking. he won't shoot.*

"How did you find me?" she asked, forcing a note of admiration into her voice, struggling not to gag on it.

"One of your so-called friends turned you in. She called the hotline. Said you were helping her get ready for a tag sale and seemed pretty anxious to get rid of some old newspaper clipping without her seeing it. When she looked, she recognized you and Tommy."

Tommy.

How she hated that name. The Murdocks had always used it, though. From the moment her son was born. She could never let him go back there. Never let him be exposed to those people and the lies they would feed him.

"You thought you could leave, didn't you, Katie? You were planning to get out of here before I found you. Looks like you're stuck now, though, doesn't it?"

"What do you want from me?" she bit out, feeling hysteria rising within her.

"I want you to do what you should have done long ago. Hand over Tommy. He's my brother's son."

"He's my son, too."

"Do you think that matters? After what you did to Thomas? You killed him, Katie."

"He killed himself. He was too big a coward to face the responsibility for what he had done to me and T.J. He killed himself, and you know it."

"You drove him to it. You have to pay for that, Katie. You can't rob our family of both Thomas and his son. Tommy is all we have. He's our future."

"No!" Olivia flung at him, not caring about the gun pointed at her, forgetting her vow to remain calm. "He isn't yours. He's my child, and he'll stay with me."

"You really believe that? You think any court will give you custody after what you've done?"

"It won't be up to a court to decide, Gregory. I won't let it get that far."

"Neither will I," he said with chilling detachment. "I can't take any chances, and I won't let this thing drag out forever. The negative publicity would kill my parents. There's only one way to get Tommy back where he belongs without any complications."

He leveled the gun at her, holding it with two hands and aiming.

"You really think you can get away with killing me in cold blood?" she asked.

"Of course I can. It was self-defense."

"Self-defense?"

"This is Thomas's gun. It was registered to him. He kept it in the house where you lived," he said with maddening composure. "As far as anyone knows, you took it with you when you ran off with Tommy. I'm wearing gloves. My prints won't be on it. You're wanted for kidnapping my nephew. When I confronted you, you pulled the gun on me. We struggled. It went off," he concluded in a matter-of-fact tone that had won many a legal battle in the courtroom.

"Naturally, as Tommy's closest living relatives, my parents will become his guardians. Don't worry, Katie. We'll all take good care of him."

Panic ambushed Olivia. She was trapped. There was no way out. If she turned to run, he'd shoot her in the back.

A sob escaped her throat as she squeezed her eyes shut and thought of T.J.

And Max.

A sound startled her.

Not the gunshot she had anticipated.

No, it was a car door opening.

T.J.'s voice shouting, "Mom!"

"T.J., no!" she screamed, turning to see that he'd stepped out of the Explorer and was staring, wild-eyed, at the man with the gun.

Shock turned to cunning recognition on Gregory's face as he spoke to the little boy. "Tommy, it's me, your uncle Greg."

Perplexed, T.J. only stared at him.

"Your mommy has done a terrible thing. I managed to get the gun away from her, but we have to be careful. You'll have to come with me, now. Go get into the truck."

"No!" T.J. shouted. "Mom, what's he talking about?"

Before Olivia could speak, another sound reached her ears.

It was the distant sound of a motor.

A car was approaching on the road, coming from the direction of Max's place.

Gregory looked around wildly, then leapt into motion. He moved forward and grabbed T.J. in one swift movement.

Olivia shrieked as her son let out a startled, frightened cry.

"Put him down!" she bellowed at Gregory, who dumped a squirming T.J. into the passenger's side of the pickup truck and climbed in after him.

Then he turned and aimed the gun at Olivia again, firing out the open window of the pickup.

There was no time to duck, no time to react.

The bullet missed her.

Gregory aimed again.

This time, she ducked. She flung herself onto the ground, rolling down an incline behind the Explorer.

The car engine was coming closer.

The pickup roared to life, taking off down the road toward town.

"T.J.!" Olivia screamed, frantic. "T.J.!"

The sound was muffled in the snow, lost in the fading echo of the truck's motor.

Max found her there, sobbing, stammering out her story. When he realized what had happened, the wind was knocked right out of him. It was as though he had been hit by a falling tree.

He held her, silent, knowing there was nothing he

could say to her, and all he could think was that he was
too late.

Too late.

He couldn't believe it.

The bastard had tried to kill her, had stolen T.J. away
from her, and it was Max's fault. If he had gotten here
even a minute sooner, he could have stopped it from happening.

Conscious of the gun in the pocket of his parka, he
knew what he would have done if he had come upon the
scene Olivia had described.

Rage pumped through his veins. If he ever came face
to face with Gregory Murdock, if he ever had the chance
to use the gun on him—

"Max, please," Olivia moaned, pulling back to look up
into his face. "Please get T.J. back. Please."

"I will. I promise," Max told her, his mind spinning.
He used the thumb of his glove to wipe the tears from
her ruddy, chapped face. "Calm down now, okay?"

"How are you going to get him back?"

"We have to call Andy."

"Andy?" she asked blankly, and then recognition appeared on her face. "Andy. You mean the police."

He nodded.

She contemplated that.

"It's the only way, Olivia," he said gently.

"I know." Resigned, tears still streaming from her eyes,
she told him, "I'm going to go to jail when they find out
who I am, Max. You know that, don't you? But I don't
care. As long as you get T.J. back from that maniac, I
don't care."

"You won't go to jail, Olivia," he said with a confidence
he didn't feel. "I'll make sure of it."

She shrugged, no longer listening. She pulled away

from him and started walking back to the Explorer, looking small and alone in the snow.

He hurried to catch up to her, wading through snow up to his knees.

"We can't take the Explorer, Olivia," he reminded her gently. "We'll never get it out of here. The snow's too deep."

She nodded dully without looking at him. She allowed him to take her arm and guide her back to Sarah's big white car.

When they were inside, the heat blasting, he wasted no time starting the engine and heading back toward his house.

"Shouldn't you head toward town?" she asked. "He went that way. Maybe we can catch up and—"

"No." He shook his head. "Not in this car. The tires are no good in the snow. They're long gone by now, Olivia."

She sobbed at those words, and he wanted to kick himself.

"It won't take long to get back to my place and call the police," he said reassuringly. "They'll set up road blocks. They'll find him."

"What if something happens to T.J. before they do?"

"T.J. is the whole reason Murdock was here, remember, Olivia?" Max pointed out. "Why would he ever want to hurt him? He thinks he's doing the right thing, and that you were wrong to take him away from the family. In his mind, he's not running from the cops. He's simply bringing T.J. home."

"He has a gun," Olivia told him flatly. "T.J. is his hostage. That's the only way to look at it, Max. And don't ever assume that he won't hurt my son. I know him, remember? He's got a history of violence. If T.J. says anything that makes him angry—" She choked, unable to continue speaking.

Max took one hand off the wheel and reached out to pat her arm, then quickly replaced it, needing to steer on the treacherous road. "It'll be okay, Olivia."

She was silent.

She didn't believe it.

He wished he did.

But he knew that, despite what Gregory Murdock had done, the facts remained essentially the same. In the eyes of the law, she was wrong. She had deliberately violated a court order and taken her son away. She had concealed her identity and lived on the lam for five years.

It was her word against Murdock's, and if his family was as influential as she claimed, she was in trouble.

Max couldn't let Olivia know that his frame of mind was pessimistic. She had to maintain hope. She had to believe that Gregory would be found, that she'd get T.J. back, that she wouldn't be arrested.

That this whole mess can be straightened out at last, Max acknowledged, and with that came another thought.

If everything else really did happen—if Gregory were put in jail and T.J. were returned to Olivia and the kidnapping charges were dropped—would one other twist on the happy ending be too much to hope for?

What if Olivia stayed in Newberry Cove . . .

What if Max asked her to be his wife?

No. It would never happen. Not in a million years.

Even if everything else worked out, he wouldn't marry her. He couldn't.

He had sworn he wouldn't allow himself to fall in love with her. Love only led to heartache, and he'd had enough of that to last a lifetime.

No, love was a distraction he didn't need. He had promised himself that he would devote his life to raising his children, and raising them right. He would do for them what his father hadn't been able to do for him and Tessa. What Sam and Lindsey's own mother hadn't been able to do for them.

He owed his children a stable home life.

Marrying a woman like Olivia, with a past like hers, was out of the question and he had known it all along.

All he could do for her now was get her son back alive and make sure the bastard who had done this to her was punished.

He slowed the car as the familiar lane appeared ahead. They were almost home. He carefully steered the car up the driveway leading to his house, intent only on the matter at hand.

Olivia paced to the window and looked out.

The snow had stopped at last. Dusk was falling. The trees that rimmed the small cabin were sagging beneath the burden of snow, casting long blue-gray shadows across the white landscape.

T.J. was out there someplace, Olivia thought bleakly. Was he afraid? Did he believe the lies Gregory had surely told him? Did he feel betrayed by her now that he knew the secret of his past?

"T.J. loves you, you know, Olivia."

Max spoke behind her, and she turned, startled, to see him watching her.

"How did you know what I was thinking?" she asked.

"Because I'm thinking the same thing. That Murdock's going to do his best to turn him against you, because everything depends on that. But T.J.'s a levelheaded kid. He won't fall for it, Olivia. He knows who he is—"

"No, he doesn't. He thinks his name is T.J. Halloran.

He thinks my name is Olivia Halloran. He has no idea who we really are or where we came from."

"But he trusts you. Nothing is going to change that. Not even Murdock's lies."

"Where do you think they are?" she asked, turning away from the window, hugging herself as she returned to the couch and the fire he had built in the hearth just for something to do.

"I don't know. They can't have gotten far on these roads," Max told her.

She stared into the fire. She couldn't feel its warmth, could feel nothing but the aching void that had settled over her in the past few hours.

In the kitchen, the teakettle whistled.

Sarah had insisted on making her a cup of camomile, insisting it would calm her nerves—as though anything could. But the woman meant well.

Olivia appreciated her bustling presence, the way she looked out for the Rothwells. Her primary function seemed to be taking care of Sam and Lindsey, keeping them upstairs and occupied so that they were away from the action downstairs.

There had been several police officers here earlier, but now only Andy remained.

Olivia knew that he wasn't here just out of friendship to Max. No, he was also here because he was duty-bound to keep an eye on her. Kidnapping was a federal offense.

Federal officers had been alerted and would arrive as soon as the roads were passable, which she realized shouldn't be long now that the snow had stopped.

Still, a phone call from the local police a short time ago had revealed that they still couldn't get through to Dr. Klimek's clinic, which they had been trying to do for hours. A tree had fallen across the road in the high winds.

Now the authorities were waiting for snowmobiles so that they could get around it.

Olivia didn't want to think about the kindly old doctor, or why the police had been unable to reach him by phone at the clinic or his home. She couldn't bear any additional painful speculation.

She wondered dully what would happen to her when the federal agents got here. Would they take her into custody immediately? Would they question her? Would they simply throw her in jail? How would she know what was going on with T.J.? Would they allow her to keep in contact?

Max had called a lawyer he knew down in Portland— Charles Downing, an old friend from his college days. The man had promised to come as soon as he could; but he, too, was snowed in. Olivia had spoken briefly to him on the phone. Charles had advised her to say nothing if she were questioned.

"But what if I can tell them something that can help lead them to T.J.?" she asked.

"Say nothing," Charles repeated. "You don't want to incriminate yourself. I'll be there as soon as I can."

Olivia knew that she had to tell the authorities anything they wanted to know, regardless of whether she was incriminating herself. If she told the truth, it might help them to find her son; and as far as she was concerned, nothing else mattered.

She glanced at Andy, who sat quietly in a chair across the room, his chin in his hand.

Under different circumstances, the might have liked Sarah's tall, soft-spoken son who so obviously held Max and his children in great affection.

But Andy was the enemy. She couldn't forget that. She had broken the law, and his job was to make sure she went to jail.

"You okay?" Max asked softly, reaching out to touch her sleeve.

She flinched. "No."

No, she wasn't okay.

She wanted to cry, to scream, to run.

To do something, *anything* other than sit here waiting.

Sarah brought her the steaming mug of tea.

Olivia murmured her thanks and sat holding it, her icy hands impervious to the heat. She heard Sarah go upstairs, heard Sam and Lindsey asking questions, heard Sarah expertly evading difficult answers.

Max drummed his fingertips on the arm of the couch.

Andy sat still and silent.

She got up to pace again, aware of Andy's wary stare and Max's concern.

She was going to go crazy.

She couldn't take this agony.

She kept seeing T.J. squirming in Gregory Murdock's grasp, kept hearing him screaming for her as Murdock dumped him into the pickup truck.

The phone rang.

Everyone jumped.

Olivia's heart raced as Andy exchanged glances with Max, then got up to answer it.

Max stood and walked over to Olivia.

"What?" she asked in dread, looking from Max to Andy, who was picking up the phone. "What is it?"

"Just wait; he'll tell us," Max said, putting his hands on her arms to steady her.

She realized she'd been swaying, that she felt dizzy. She leaned on Max, hating that she needed his support.

She shouldn't need him. She had no right.

"When?" Andy was saying into the phone, his tone all business.

Olivia watched him carefully, trying to discern some expression in his face, but there was none.

"Where did it happen?" Andy asked.

"What happened?" Olivia burst out, trying to wriggle from Max's grasp. But he held her, and she squirmed. "Let go of me," she snapped at him.

"Just wait, Olivia," Max said.

She hated the calming tone of his voice, hated the dread she could see in his eyes despite it. He was worried, dammit. He didn't really believe that T.J. would come home safely. He knew that something had happened, knew that Andy was hearing about it right now. He knew that her entire world was about to be shattered, and all he could say was *just wait*.

"Let go!" she flung at him through clenched teeth.

But he wouldn't.

He just held her; and the harder she tried to pull away, the closer he pulled her until she was up against his chest, her face against his fleece pullover.

Andy had lowered his voice, but still his words were audible.

"What about the boy?" he was asking.

A moan escaped Olivia. She strained to hear the voice on the other end of the phone, strained to turn her head and look at Andy's expression, but Max wouldn't let her. Max had imprisoned her in his arms and he wouldn't let go.

Did he think he could protect her? Was that it?

"All right," Andy was saying. "All right. I'll be waiting." Then he hung up.

"What happened?" Max asked him.

In that moment, Olivia allowed herself to go limp in his arms.

Suddenly, she didn't want to know whatever it was that

Andy had just been told. She couldn't bear to hear the words. Something had happened to T.J. She knew it.

"Murdock's dead."

Olivia gasped.

"Dead?" Max echoed. Stunned, he released his grip on her.

Dazed, she turned her head toward Andy, saw that he was nodding.

"How?" Max asked.

Olivia couldn't speak.

"His truck went off the road on a curve. Flipped over on the embankment."

A high-pitched wail filled the room. At first, Olivia didn't even realize that it was coming from her own throat. When she did, it erupted into hysterical sobbing.

Max held her.

This time, she didn't struggle.

Murdock had been killed in an accident. That meant that T.J. . . .

". . . wasn't with him."

Andy's words reached her through a fog of grief She blinked.

"Did you hear what he said, Olivia?" Max was saying. "T.J. wasn't in the car with him. T.J. wasn't killed, Olivia."

Stunned, she looked from Max to Andy, who nodded.

"But where . . ." she whispered, dazed.

"Nobody knows. Murdock was alone in the truck. It happened about ten miles south of here along the coastal highway."

For a moment, Olivia allowed herself to hope that T.J. might be alive.

Then she saw the bleak expressions on Andy's and Max's faces.

The harsh reality settled in, and she knew the truth. There could only be one reason T.J. wasn't in the truck.

Gregory must have already done something to him and gotten rid of the evidence.

Oh, God.

"Oh, *God*," Olivia whimpered, and felt her legs give way.

"How is she?" Andy asked when Max returned from the bedroom.

"How do you think she is?" Max asked curtly. "Your mother is going to stay with her. She's trying to calm her."

"Look, I know you're angry, Max, but don't direct it at me," Andy said quietly.

"You're sitting here keeping tabs on her like she's the Son of Sam, Andy," Max accused, picking up another log and throwing it carelessly on the fire, resulting in a shower of sparks.

"I'm only doing my job," Andy pointed out. "I have no choice."

"I know," Max said, suddenly resigned. "I'm just frustrated beyond belief, Andy. Her kid is out there somewhere—with any luck. With any luck, he managed to get away somehow and that's why he wasn't in the truck when Murdock crashed."

"Do you really believe that?"

"No," Max said heavily.

Tears sprang to his eyes.

He could hear Sam and Lindsey playing a video game upstairs. He swallowed over the lump in his throat and asked Andy, "What's going to happen when the federal agents get here?"

"What do you think?"

"She did what she had to do for her kid's sake, Andy. Murdock is a monster, and so was his brother."

"Then you should have faith, Max, that the courts won't see fit to punish her for what she did."

"How can I have faith in that? There's no evidence against Murdock."

"She says he took the kid away from her against his will."

"Without her son around to say it, there's no proof of that." He puffed his cheeks out and exhaled. "Murdock could have been trying to rescue the kid from his crazed mother who kidnapped him out of spite for the family after her husband dumped her. That's the defense the family will use, Andy. There's no one to come to her defense."

"You can, Max."

"What's that going to do for her? I haven't known her more than a few weeks. And I wasn't there today when Murdock ambushed her. I didn't witness what happened."

"Do you believe her?"

Max stared at Andy. "Of course I do."

"Maybe the judge will, too."

"Yeah." Max rubbed his temples, then buried his forehead in his hands. "It doesn't even matter anymore, Andy. I know her. Without her son, she won't care what happens to her. She won't fight."

"Maybe she will."

"Why bother? What does she have without T.J.?"

"You. Sam. Lindsey."

"No," Max said forcefully. "We've got no future together, Andy. We already knew that before any of this happened."

"Why not?"

Max hesitated. He couldn't even remember why not. His mind was too cluttered with other thoughts; fogged with the sorrow over the loss of T.J.

"I don't know why not," he said finally, truthfully. "Look, I'm going to go check on her. I want to stay with her awhile. Do me a favor."

"What?"

"When those agents get here, explain the situation. Tell them she's not going anywhere, but that she needs some time to get herself together. See if they'll go easy on her."

"Max, I don't think—"

"Just try, Andy," he said sharply. "Just try, okay?"

With that, he went into the bedroom.

Olivia was huddled beneath the quilt, her knees drawn up against her chest, her arms wrapped tightly around her legs. Her face was gaunt and tear-streaked.

Sarah sat beside her on the bed. She looked up when Max entered.

Olivia didn't move. She just stared off into space, her expression desolate, her eyes puffy and vacant.

"I'll sit with her for a while, Sarah," Max said. "Will you go up and get the kids ready for bed? Tell them I'll come kiss them good night in a little while."

"All right. You should rest, too," Sarah told him.

"Rest? I can't. I have to be with her."

"I know." She cast a look at Olivia and touched her hand lightly. "I'm here if you need me, honey," she said tenderly.

Olivia barely nodded.

Sarah left, shaking her head sadly and closing the door behind her.

Max perched carefully on the edge of the bed.

"Did they find him yet?" she asked dully, not looking at Max.

Startled, he fumbled for a response. Did she really think T.J. was still alive?

"His body, I mean," she said in that same monotone.

"Olivia—"

"I know he's gone, Max."

"You don't know that. He might have gotten away. Or Gregory might have left him someplace."

"Why would he do that?"

"I don't know. But as long as we don't know where he is, we have to hope he'll be found."

"You don't really think he will, do you?"

It was a statement, not a question.

It took every ounce of energy Max possessed to say, "I don't know what's going to happen, Olivia. But there's always hope."

She shook her head, but said nothing.

He wanted to hold her, but sensed that if he touched her now, she'd recoil.

So, he simply sat beside her, in silence, as the dark night wore on.

THIRTEEN

Olivia woke to the sound of a ringing telephone.

Disoriented, she looked around and realized where she was.

The memory of today's horror slammed into her and she gasped, wondering how she could ever have fallen asleep.

She saw Max lying beside her, huddled on his side, and, looking out the window, realized that it was still night. The sky looked black and was shrouded in clouds.

In the next room, the telephone had stopped ringing and she heard Andy's voice murmuring, too low to be heard.

Carefully, she slipped out of bed. Max didn't stir. She watched him sleeping for a moment and realized she was stretching a hand toward his head, as though she'd been about to smooth his hair.

She couldn't touch him.

She didn't dare.

Not now. Not ever again.

She walked into the living room.

Andy looked up from the telephone receiver he'd just replaced.

"Olivia," he said, and from his tone and the expression on his face, she knew he had bad news.

"Oh, no, please," she breathed, feeling her legs go liquid again.

It was T.J.

She knew it.

They'd found his body.

"My baby," she wailed.

Andy walked over to her, took her arm. He was talking, but she couldn't hear what he was saying. Her mind was consumed by her grief. She kept sobbing T.J.'s name, aching for the child she had loved more than life itself.

"Olivia," Andy said forcefully as he held her arm and shook her a little, then harder. "Olivia, are you listening to me? Listen to me!"

"No!" she hurled at him, delirious, trying to get up, to run away.

And then Max was there, holding her.

Max and Andy were talking.

Through it all, she sobbed.

Until Max grabbed her face, cupping it in his hands, and shouted at her, "It wasn't T.J. Olivia, he wasn't talking about T.J."

Tremors of shock zapped her into silence. She could only stare at Max, trying to comprehend.

"Do you understand, Olivia? It wasn't T.J.," Max said again.

Relief slipped in, along with confusion. She had heard Andy say something about finding a body, about someone being shot. She had been so certain it was T.J.

Finally, she found her voice. "Then . . . who?"

Max looked at Andy.

The police officer motioned for him to tell her.

"Dr. Klimek," Max said.

"Oh . . . oh, no," she moaned.

So, it wasn't her son. And maybe she had known this was coming, deep down. But still it was a staggering blow.

Max held her as she cried for the old man, knowing he had lost his life because of her. She hated Gregory Murdock with every ounce of her being. There was no consolation in the knowledge that he was dead, that he would never bother her again. She had lost too much at his hands—everything. She had lost everything.

"It's going to be all right, Olivia."

Max's words reached her ears and she pulled back in disbelief.

"All right?" she echoed, vaguely noting that Andy had discreetly left them alone. "How can you say that?"

"I'm sorry, I—"

"It's never going to be all right, Max. I'm going to go to jail."

"No, you won't. I'll do everything I can to help you. Charles—"

"Max, there's nothing you can do, or Charles, and I don't even want anybody to try. I have nothing to live for. I might as well be locked away for the rest of my life."

"You do have something to live for," he contradicted.

"What?" she demanded. "What do I possibly have to live for?"

His response caught her off guard.

"Me," he said quietly. "And Sam. And Lindsey."

"No. Max, no . . . I can't. I don't want that. You don't either. This doesn't change anything."

"Yes, it does. It changes everything. Murdock isn't out there anymore, lurking. You don't have to spend your life running. You need us, Olivia. And we need you."

"No. I need my son," she said resolutely. "I never should have taken a chance. If I had kept going the way I was, keeping to myself, he never would have found us. T.J. would still be here."

"Listen, Olivia, you can't blame yourself for what's happened. And you can't blame me. I'm not the one who called and tipped off Murdock. You could have trusted me."

"But I didn't." She stared at him. "I was afraid to trust you. I was afraid to get involved because it would mean letting my guard down. The minute I did—the minute I let you into my life—it all fell apart. And now T.J.—"

"You don't know where T.J. is, Olivia," Max said again. "You have no way of knowing where he is. The police are combing the area for him now. He might still be alive."

"We both know that he probably isn't."

Max didn't reply.

"Where's Andy?" she asked abruptly, pulling away from him and looking around.

"In the kitchen. Why?"

"I want to turn myself in now and get it over with."

"Olivia, come on, you can't—"

"Max, just—just go away and leave me alone," she said harshly, and turned her back on him.

She hated herself for what she was doing to him, but she couldn't help it. She couldn't go on as though nothing had happened. She couldn't plan a future with him as though she were going to go free, as though the past weren't going to haunt her for the rest of her days.

She had never felt more alone in her life.

She ached for her precious child, her T.J., who had depended on his mommy to take care of him. She had let him down.

"I'm so sorry, baby," she sobbed.

Behind her, Max touched her shoulders.

She jerked away. "Get away from me!" she shouted.

He took his hands off her but didn't move.

She was quaking, aching, falling apart. She wanted

nothing more than to make the pain go away. But it hung over her, strangling every shred of hope.

Eventually, Max left, walking into the bedroom again and slamming the door behind him.

Max jabbed the shovel into the crusted snow and lifted an impossibly weighty chunk of it, flinging it over his shoulder onto the growing pile behind him.

It was a waste of time, really, to clear the walk in front of the door. Though several inches of new snow had fallen over night on top of what was already there, temperatures were predicted to rise today. By midafternoon, it would be well into the forties and stay there overnight. By tomorrow morning, this stuff would be melted.

But Max needed the labor, needed something to do. He couldn't spend another day pacing around the house, waiting for the phone to ring, trying to occupy the twins, who were asking too many uncomfortable questions about Olivia—and T.J. They didn't know exactly what was going on, but they suspected something was terribly wrong.

It had been almost forty-eight hours now since T.J. had disappeared into the snow with Gregory Murdock.

Almost twenty-four hours since Olivia had been driven away by the two federal authorities who had finally made it through the snow to Max's house.

He had stayed in his room while they were taking her away—partly, he was ashamed to admit even to himself, out of anger.

He didn't want to resent her for the things she had said to him. He knew she was grieving, that she'd been through hell. How could he have expected her to change her mind about him at a time like that? Had he really thought she would look at him and tell him that she loved him?

He hadn't said it to her.

Because he hadn't known how he felt.

Did he love her?

Hell, how could he tell? He'd thought he loved Julia so long ago, and look what had happened there.

Did it matter whether he loved Olivia?

No.

Not when she felt that she had nothing to live for. He had been a fool to try and convince her that she had a future with him and the twins. He didn't even know why he'd said it, except that the words had just popped out and he couldn't seem to help himself. He wanted to help her, to make her hurt go away, to take care of her . . . forever.

In that moment, he had thought that it was possible.

He should have known better. Hadn't he told himself all along that he didn't want a woman in his life? He didn't want a stepmother for the twins. There was too much potential for pain, for loss . . .

He couldn't stand more pain. More loss.

So many people had been stolen from Max's life. His mother. His father. Tessa. Julia. And now T.J. . . .

The thought of the little boy overwhelmed him with sorrow. He buried his head in his hands and wondered how she could bear it.

Maybe Olivia was right. Maybe she would be better off spending the rest of her life in jail after all. If anything ever happened to his children, he knew he wouldn't care what happened to him.

Charles had called last night.

He had said he was with her, that he would do every-thing he could to see that justice was served. But he couldn't make any promises. Not without some hard evidence against Murdock.

"Hard evidence?" Max had echoed incredulously. "What about Joe Klimek's murdered body?"

"I'm working on that," Charles said. "Without a weapon that we can trace to Murdock—"

"There's no weapon?"

"They couldn't find one in the wreckage of the car, and there was nothing at the scene," Charles said. "Some prints were lifted from an open file-cabinet drawer that could place him there, but without a weapon . . ."

"Keep me posted," Max had told him tersely before hanging up.

So, Murdock might have gotten away with murder.

The fact that he'd been killed doing so was of little solace to Max.

He continued to shovel, wondering when the twins were going to wake up. He wanted to be inside when they did. It was just past seven now, and they had been sound asleep when he'd checked them before coming out here.

He heard a car's engine in the distance and looked up. Was someone approaching? Or was it simply someone passing by?

There was very little traffic on the dirt road under any circumstances at this time of year. Besides his house, there was nothing out this way but a few boarded-up summer cottages. At this hour, on a snowy morning, who would be passing by?

He realized the car was drawing nearer, that it was approaching on his driveway. So. Somebody was coming to see him.

He leaned on the upright handle of the shovel, watching the drive through narrowed eyes. His heart was pounding, but he refused to let himself think the worst.

Not even when the car emerged from the trees and he

saw that it was a police cruiser, and that it belonged to Andy.

He stood, silent and waiting, as Andy parked a few yards away and opened the door.

"Max," he said, walking toward him.

"What are you doing here?"

"I wanted to come out and tell you in person."

Max clenched his hands on the shovel's handle, not sure whether they ached from the cold seeping through his gloves or the tension in his grip; but he didn't relax, and he didn't move.

"Tell me what?" he asked Andy.

"They found the kid."

It was what he'd been expecting.

Yet the news stole Max's voice, his composure, his breath. He crumpled, letting go of the shovel and sinking to the ground, crouching there, holding his head.

"No," Andy said, touching his shoulder. "No, Max, not like that. They found the kid. Alive, Max. The kid is alive!"

Max looked up, incredulous. "Alive? They found him alive? T.J.?"

Andy nodded, grinning.

Max opened his mouth to speak but released only a sob.

"He was in the woods," Andy said. "Hiding."

"What woods? Where?"

"A few miles up the coast. He said that when Murdock swerved to miss hitting a deer, the truck spun out. Murdock had to get out to push it. When he did, the kid grabbed the gun and ran."

"He left the gun in the truck with the kid?" Max asked, smirking. Inside, he was rejoicing, shouting, *Good for you, T.J.!*

"Guess he must have panicked. The guy wasn't used

to driving in the snow. He was from Southern Cal, remember?"

Max smirked again. "So, T.J. took the gun and ran?"

Andy nodded. "Into the woods. It was snowing pretty
hard. He kept going."

"Didn't Murdock go after him?"

"He must have. But he didn't get him."

"Thank God," Max said, wiping at the tears he couldn't
keep from his eyes.

He looked at Andy and saw that he was misty, too. Good
old Andy.

"The kid was lost in the woods until late last night. He
kept walking and stumbled across a house. If he hadn't,
I don't want to think about what would have happened,
Max. He could have been lost out there for—"

"But he's all right?" Max asked anxiously.

"Frostbit. But all right. Turned the gun over. They're
going to match the bullet that killed Klimek with it. When
they do, they'll have proof that Murdock was the one who
murdered him."

"What if the family tries to pin it on Olivia?" Max
asked.

"They can try; but with T.J. as a witness, they won't get
away with it. He'll tell the truth about what happened.
The kid was scared out of his mind. Kept talking about
how the bad man tried to shoot his mommy."

"Christ," Max muttered, trying to force the disturbing
image from his mind.

Olivia could have been killed. T.J., too.

They were both safe.

They weren't here with him, but they were out of danger.

He tried to convince himself that that was all that mattered.

* * *

"Olivia?"

She looked up to see Charles standing in the doorway of the small room to which she had been escorted a few minutes ago. Only a few hours had passed since he had come to give her the most joyous news she had ever received.

Now he was back, and her heart was pounding in trepidation. Had something happened?

Had they been wrong about T.J.? Had there been some mistake? Was he . . . ?

"What happened?" she asked, watching his face for some sign.

"I have wonderful news," he told her.

"Wonderful news?" she echoed, puzzled. The only wonderful news that mattered was the news he had already told her.

Her child was alive.

Nothing could top that.

Except . . .

"The Murdocks have dropped the charges against you, Olivia."

Her head swimming in disbelief, she could only stare.

"Apparently, they have decided they'd rather not stir up the publicity this case would create. Gregory's death is already too much of a scandal."

"My God," she breathed, shaking her head. "They've dropped the charges. So that means—"

"You have nothing left to worry about, Olivia," Charles said, smiling at her. "You can go home and raise your son."

"I can go home," she repeated, scarcely able to believe it.

It wasn't until later, when she was on her way to the hospital and a reunion with T.J., that she realized what had happened when Charles had said that.

You can go home.

The image that had come to her mind wasn't of the ramshackle farmhouse where she and T.J. had lived in solitude these past few years.

No, she had immediately thought of Max's cozy cabin.

Well, that wasn't home and it never would be.

She had her son back and she had her freedom. That was more than she had ever dared to hope for. Anything more would be . . .

Impossible.

Just as she had always known it would.

She wasn't the Queen of the World, and this was no fairy tale. She couldn't marry Max and live happily after.

He didn't love her.

He wanted to protect her, yes. He felt responsible for her for some reason. But back before things had grown so complicated, he had said that he didn't want to get married again. She couldn't let herself forget that . . . even if her own circumstances had changed.

Now there was nothing standing in her way. She could step out of the shadows and live her life the way she wanted. She could even fall in love, get married . . .

If she wanted.

Maybe someday, someone would come along who could make her forget the nightmare of the past. Maybe even make her forget Max.

No, she corrected herself fiercely.

That was impossible. Nobody would ever make her forget Max. Nobody.

She found herself starting to think, *If only—*

But she couldn't do that. No more *if onlys*. She had everything she needed. She would be a fool to hope for more than that.

FOURTEEN

"Hey, Mom, look at me!"

"I see you, but—please be careful, T.J.!" Olivia called, skating over to his side as he executed a wobbly jump and spin on the small skates she'd bought for him last Christmas. Just a little over a year ago, yet it seemed like another lifetime.

How many lifetimes had she lived? she wondered as she watched her son push off again and go gliding smoothly along the thick ice that covered the small woodland pond behind their rented farmhouse.

There had been her childhood as Katie Kenrick.

And then the years she had spent with Thomas as Katie Murdock.

After that, she was Olivia Halloran, furtively hiding herself and her son from the world in an effort to escape the past.

And now . . .

Who was she?

Who had she become in the two months that had passed since Gregory had been killed and T.J. had been found alive and the Murdocks had miraculously dropped the charges?

She wasn't sure.

All she knew was that her days had resumed a certain

rhythm, and for that, she was grateful. She and T.J. continued to live in the old run-down farmhouse that might not be home in the long run, but was familiar territory for the time being. After what they had been through, she understood the need to cling to anything familiar, for her own sake and for her son's. In time she would consider leaving the old house, probably even leaving Newberry Cove, although for some reason, she couldn't quite bring herself to consider that drastic a step. Not yet.

No, right now all she could do was stay busy so that she and T.J. could heal.

So, she got up in the morning and made breakfast for the two of them before T.J. went to school. Oatmeal, usually, at T.J.'s request. With brown sugar. But she didn't make a raisin face in his bowl, and he didn't ask her to.

After breakfast, when her son was safely deposited at school, she headed over to the clinic, just as she always had.

To her shock, Dr. Klimek had left everything to her and T.J. His house, his business, and all his worldly goods.

He had updated his will in the months before his death. As it turned out, he had no family; and if Gregory Murdock's gun hadn't ended his life on that snowy November morning, cancer would inevitably have cut it short very soon. The autopsy had shown the deadly tumor.

That didn't make his passing any easier on Olivia and T.J. Only when he was gone did she realize how much affection she'd had for the old man.

It helped to go to the clinic every morning and keep things running smoothly. She wasn't a doctor, but she was a technician and she could tend to many of the animals' needs. Those she couldn't help, she referred to the new veterinarian who had opened an office several towns over. For now, she didn't know what she'd do with Dr.

Klimek's business. But it was therapeutic, helping the sick and wounded animals—for her—and for T.J., who was quieter than usual lately.

Which was to be expected.

Olivia wondered how long it would be before he was his old self again—whether he ever would be. He didn't like to talk about what had happened, though he had said Gregory Murdock hadn't hurt him, and as far as he could tell, hadn't intended to. But so far he hadn't told Olivia what Murdock had said to him in those terrifying hours while he was his captive.

She had a pretty good idea, though.

Whatever it was, it hadn't changed T.J.'s feelings about her. She would never forget how his face had lit up when she saw him lying in that hospital bed, his little face still burned red from the raging wind and snow.

"Mom!" he'd yelled when he saw her in the doorway.

As she rushed to him and held him, sobbing in relief and joy, she had told herself that for the rest of her life she would never need anything but this. To have her child with her, safe and healthy.

That was all it would take to make her life complete.

Except . . .

Now that her days had settled back into a routine, she couldn't help feeling wistful. She hated herself for allowing the slightest hint of discontentment to steal its way over her, but there were times when she just couldn't help it.

Mostly it happened late at night, when she lay in her bed listening to T.J.'s even breathing in the next room and the wind howling around the house. She felt alone, then. Lonely.

She thought of Max.

Had he heard that the charges had been cleared and she was still in town? The story had been in the papers, of course. But Max didn't read them. He had told her that it was easier to be happy when you were unaware of the tragedies unfolding in the world. He didn't want to know about starving children or weapons inspections or an unstable economy.

"But don't you think it's important to know what's going on?" Olivia had asked him, incredulous. "For your children's sake, at least?"

"No," Max had said stubbornly. "For their sake, I don't want to know. I want to shelter them from all that as much as I possibly can."

She thought about that often these days—about the isolated life he had built for himself and the twins. Was he any different, really, than she had been for so many years? Living the way he did, a virtual recluse, keeping the children out of school and away from people who might hurt them.

Well, it seemed to Olivia that his sacrifices might ultimately turn out to have been made in vain. You could do everything in your power to stay safe, to shield yourself and your children from harm, to forget a tragic past and ensure that nothing would ever hurt you again. But in the end, there were no guarantees.

Look at me, Max, she told him silently. *Look what happened to me. I couldn't hide. I couldn't escape. In the end, I couldn't even run away. But I'm okay. T.J. and I—we're going to be okay. And we won't live the rest of our lives in the shadows.*

"I'm cold, Mom," T.J. called from the other side of the pond, where he was hobbling onto the bank and bending to unlace his skates. "Let's go in and have some hot chocolate. With whipped cream *and* marshmallows, okay?"

"Okay," she called. "I'm coming."

She pushed off and sailed across the ice toward him.

She stretched her arms out on either side of her, flying, the cold wind blowing her blond-again hair.

Look at me, Max, she said again, tilting her face up to the winter sun in the pure blue sky and wiping at the tears that suddenly stung her eyes. *Look at me. I've got everything I ever wanted.*

"Can we go to school, Daddy?"

Max blinked and looked up from his cup of coffee to see his daughter staring solemnly at him.

"School?" he echoed. "What do you mean?"

"A real school," she said. "With a teacher. And a classroom. And other kids."

"This is your school, Lindsey. I'm your teacher. And you have your brother."

"Yeah," she said grumpily, glancing at Sam, who sat reading the back of the Cocoa Puffs box. "I guess."

Max sipped his coffee. Waited for her to change the subject.

When she didn't, but continued to stare moodily at him, he gave in and asked, "Why do you want to go to school?"

"Because it's lonely here," she said promptly. "Me and Sam were thinking it would be fun to go to school and have friends."

Max considered that. "What if I had Andy and Janey bring their kids over to play? Wouldn't that be fun?"

Sam looked up and made a face. "They're too little," he said.

"Yeah, they're babies," Lindsey agreed. "We want to go to school and have friends our age. And have clubs and gym class and all that stuff."

Max sighed. He had known they were restless lately.

He'd tried to tell himself it was just that time of year; blaming the season for his own restlessness, as well.

He didn't want to consider the real reason he couldn't sleep, couldn't eat, couldn't think straight these days.

"If we went to school—" Lindsey began.

"Enough." Max barked, cutting her off effectively.

She gaped at him. So did Sam.

He pushed back the guilt that rushed at him, telling himself he knew what was best for his children. Someday, they'd thank him for all he had done to make sure their lives were stable. There would be no schoolchildren taunting them about their mother, no whispers behind their backs, no drugs, no losses . . .

They would have a father who took care of them, a father who had devoted his whole life to them. Someday, when they were grown up and ready to face the world on their own, they could leave if they wanted to.

If? he questioned incredulously. *You mean when. Of course they'll want to leave. All children do. All children grow up, and then they leave home. That's how it works.*

For the first time, he allowed himself to wonder what he would do when that time came. Maybe it wasn't all that far off. Maybe, when they turned eighteen, they would choose to go to college.

Well, don't you want them to go to college? he demanded, hating the wave of misgiving that washed over him.

Sure I do. But where will that leave me? That's only twelve years off. Am I going to be left alone here in twelve years?

He looked up at Sam and Lindsey.

Sam had gone back to reading his cereal box. Lindsey was toying with the crusts of toast left on her plate, her blond head bent.

What the hell are you doing to them? Max asked himself, suddenly feeling as though he were being crushed under an overwhelming weight.

He had spent the last six years trying to shield his children from pain—or so he'd told himself.

But they were too young to remember Julia, to bear lasting scars from her neglect. They were young enough, even, that they might be unfazed by what people might say about their mother, about the way she had left, and the way she had died.

Maybe, Max thought reluctantly, what he was really trying to do was shield himself.

Maybe *he* was the one who needed to hide away from the big, bad world.

Maybe *he* was the one who couldn't deal with the truth about Julia.

And maybe *he* was the one who wouldn't bounce back from another loss.

Rather than facing what had happened in the past and putting it behind him . . .

Rather than taking chances and boldly reaching out for the future . . .

He had chosen to run, to hide.

But it hadn't worked. Despite his efforts to keep at bay life and all its potential pain, it had crept in anyway. No, not crept in.

Life had slammed him over the head.

No, he amended again, not life.

Love.

Love had happened to him.

He was in love with Olivia.

He stood abruptly and carried his coffee mug over to the sink.

"Where are you going, Daddy?" Sam asked behind him.

He stood staring unseeingly out the window at the snowy woods, gripping the edge of the counter with both hands to steady himself.

"What's wrong, Daddy?" Lindsey asked.

"Nothing," he lied. "Nothing's wrong. I'm fine."

I'm just the biggest fool who ever walked the face of the earth, Lindsey. That's all.

But it was too late to take back years of misguided efforts to protect himself and his children, wasn't it? He couldn't change what he'd done.

He couldn't change what had happened with Olivia, even if he wanted to.

Charles had told him Olivia's mother- and father-in-law had dropped the charges against her. He had seemed surprised that Max hadn't already heard.

"Didn't she tell you that herself?" Charles had asked when he stopped by on his way back to Portland.

And Max had just shrugged, unable to bring himself to say aloud that he had shut her out of his life.

For all he knew, by now, Olivia and T.J. were miles away from here. He hadn't been able to bring himself to ask about her these past few weeks—not that there was anyone to ask, he reminded himself grimly. He had effectively cut himself off from Newberry Cove and everyone in it.

Not Andy, though. Andy still came around every now and then, even though Max had turned down his invitations to spend Thanksgiving and Christmas there. He had told his old friend that the kids had colds both times; and if Andy didn't believe it, he didn't let on. Maybe he sensed that Max needed to be alone after all that had happened with Olivia and T.J.

Now Max wondered whether Andy knew anything—when Olivia and T.J. had left, or maybe even where they'd gone.

Probably not. It wasn't as though Olivia would be inclined to notify the local police if she left town.

There was always Sarah . . .

But even if Sarah were around, she wouldn't know. Olivia had bonded with her in those brief, traumatic hours, but Max knew they hadn't seen each other since. Sarah would have told him. And she had left for Cocoa Beach right after Thanksgiving. She always spent Christmas and New Year's down in Florida with her sister, and never came back until late January.

The twins had been asking for her daily, though. And no wonder. Aside from him, she was all they had. Their one link to the rest of the world.

Max turned slowly to face his small children, both sitting at the table, staring at him expectantly.

"I'm sorry, guys," he said, and paused to swallow hard over a lump that had suddenly risen in his throat.

"Sorry about what, Daddy?" Lindsey asked.

"I'm sorry we live way out here in the woods—"

"We love living in the woods!" Sam cut in. "Geez, why are you sorry about that?"

"It's not just that," Max said, then hesitated.

How could he ever explain to a couple of six-year-olds that he'd robbed them of several years of a normal, happy childhood?

That he'd denied them the chance to have a step-mother and a stepbrother—a *real* family?

He couldn't bring that up now. Not when their questions about Olivia and T.J. had finally started to subside.

In the first few days after they'd left, Sam and Lindsey had asked about them incessantly. All Max could bring himself to tell them was that Olivia and T.J. had had to move back to their old home unexpectedly. They'd cried, and they'd written letters, and he had promised to mail them just as soon as he had an address. He'd acted as though everything would be fine and Olivia and T.J. would be in touch just as soon as they got settled.

If only that were true, he told himself now.

He cleared his throat and looked from his son's puzzled expression to his daughter's worried eyes. "I'm sorry," he said again, "that I thought you shouldn't go to school in town. Maybe I was wrong."

"You were?" Sam asked.

"You mean we can go to school?" Lindsey asked, lighting up.

"I think maybe you can," Max told them. "If that's what you want."

Clearly, it was.

They were laughing, jumping around, making plans.

Max stood there and watched them, marveling at how the world seemed to have changed in an instant. The kids were going to go to school.

Maybe he, too, would venture out of the cocoon that had sheltered him these past few years. Maybe it was time to rejoin the living.

But would he ever feel fully alive again without her?

He squeezed his eyes shut and saw Olivia's face. He remembered what it had been like to hold her, to make love to her, to lie in the silent, sleeping house with her in his arms, her heart beating against his.

He had known, that last time they were together that way, that it would never happen again. He had told himself then that he would never lose the memory; he had been aware that it would be all he had left of her.

He had told himself it would have to be enough.

Now he knew it never would be.

Olivia turned the key in the lock and stepped over the threshold into the silent, unfamiliar house.

She found herself standing in a small entrance hall, the outlines of a low bench and telephone table dimly visible in the gray light spilling through the window in the door. She was careful to close the door behind her, pushing it hard to make it stick, as the realtor, Sally Knowlton, had warned her to do.

"Take anything you want to keep, and I'll arrange an estate sale for the rest when we list the house," Sally had told her. "There's no rush, though. Nobody's going to jump to buy it, especially at this time of year."

Olivia walked across the worn linoleum floor and found herself in a shabbily furnished living room. She couldn't help feeling like an intruder, even though this was technically her house and she had every right to be here.

Still, she couldn't quite grasp the reality that Dr. Klimek had left this place to her. It seemed tragic that the man had no one else, no family. What must it feel like to reach the end of your life and have nobody there to take care of you, nobody to leave things to but an employee who might as well have been a stranger?

She had never known anything about him other than what was connected to his work. Until she had visited his grave in the old church cemetery yesterday to lay some red roses there for Valentine's Day, she hadn't even known he'd once had a wife. Beth. She had died half a century ago, according to the crumbling old stone next to Dr. Klimek's.

How he must have ached when he was widowed, Olivia mused as she walked slowly through the silent living room.

Just as you ache?

No! she told herself quickly, stopping to pick up and absently examine an old leather-bound Bible lying on a table. *I didn't ache when I was widowed. Not for the loss of Thomas, anyway.*

But that hadn't been what she was thinking about.

No, she ached *now.* Because of Max.

Because not a day went by when she wasn't haunted

by thoughts of him, by a fierce longing for what they'd almost had.

She had hoped time would help to heal the pain. But here it was February, and the dull emptiness only seemed to be growing worse.

She had toyed with the idea of moving with T.J. into Dr. Klimek's house. She had even driven by it a few times and thought maybe they could live here and build a life in Newberry Cove after all.

But finally she had realized that she couldn't put down roots here. Not this way. Not with Max living so close by that she might run into him someday.

And then what?

Then they would both awkwardly fumble for small talk and sooner or later he would walk away and she would be left wanting him more than ever before.

So, she had decided that the best thing to do was to leave Newberry Cove and start over someplace else. Maybe down south. Someplace where the sun would shine and she could be warm.

She was always cold these days, she thought as she set down the Bible and shivered in the unheated old house. Always trying to warm up, with blankets and fires and tea, and nothing helped.

Maybe the southern sun wouldn't even help.

Maybe the only thing that could truly warm her was Max's arms.

Stop that! she scolded herself and moved briskly across the room.

She was going to sell this house and the business, and she was going to get out of town and never look back. Just as soon as T.J.'s school year ended in June. She had decided to wait that long to minimize the upheaval for him. She didn't want him to have to start a new school midway through the year or to leave the few tentative friends he'd managed to make in his current class.

She hadn't told him yet that they were going.

She figured she had plenty of time to break the news. She'd wait until she'd made some plans; until she had a definite destination in mind. She'd make it sound like they were setting out on an adventure, just the two of them.

Another fresh start.

She sighed wearily.

A fresh start. That was the last thing she wanted at this stage in her life.

What she wanted was to be settled. What she wanted was to be *home*. Someplace where she and T.J. belonged.

The trouble was, they didn't belong anyplace.

She wandered over to the mantel and glanced at the dusty knickknacks there. A few small china figurines, a clock . . .

And a photo.

She picked it up.

It had been taken years ago—probably the forties, judging from the clothing and hairstyle on the pretty woman smiling in black-and-white. She was sitting in the grass, surrounded by what looked like daffodils, and she was looking up with twinkling eyes at whoever had held the camera.

This must have been his wife, Olivia realized. Dr. Klimek's wife Beth, who had died so young.

She ran a fingertip over the metal frame's ornate antique scrolls, surprised to find that there was a lump in her throat.

How tragic that he had lost her, that he had spent the rest of his life alone.

I don't want that to be me, Olivia realized suddenly. *My*

God, I don't want it to be me, old and lonely and forever heart-broken.

Again she thought of Max.

Carefully, she set the picture frame back on the mantel and turned away, wiping tears from her eyes.

Max sat thrumming his fingertips against the steering wheel of the Explorer, staring through the curtain of snow flurries at the two-story red-brick building with the white-paned windows.

Newberry Cove Elementary School hadn't changed much in the twenty-something years since he'd gone here. The hand-painted sign out front was new, and the playground equipment off to the side had been updated; but other than that, it looked exactly the same.

So, why did he find it so threatening now?

Why was he holding his breath, wary, waiting for the doors to open up and spill out his two precious children?

Because he desperately needed reassurance that they had survived this, their first official day in the real world. He had done nothing but worry since he'd dropped them off here this morning.

It had taken longer than he'd expected to get them enrolled once he'd made the decision to do so. First, there had to be meetings with the school officials and teachers, doctor's visits and vaccinations, placement testing. Then—thanks to all the unaccustomed exposure to civilization, no doubt—they'd both come down with the flu, followed immediately by chicken pox.

Finally, this third week in February, their scars faded to faint red marks here and there, the children were ready, and more than willing. They had skipped away with their brand-new bookbags and lunch boxes without a backward glance at Max, and he'd tried to convince himself that was a good thing.

He hadn't known what to do with himself after that. He'd driven around aimlessly, not quite able to bring himself to go back to the silent house without them. He'd run a few errands, then stopped at Sarah's and shoveled her walk, staying for lunch when she insisted.

She'd told him he was doing the right thing sending the kids to school. It was what he needed to hear.

"You can't lock them away forever, Max," she'd said, setting a basket of fresh rolls in front of him, along with a steaming bowl of homemade minestrone.

"I know, Sarah. I finally figured that out."

"Did you figure out anything else while you were at it?"

He'd looked at her through narrowed eyes. "Like what?"

She'd shrugged. "If you don't know what I'm talking about, I guess I have my answer."

He'd feigned incomprehension—and disinterest. Changed the subject. Pretended that Olivia wasn't on his mind the rest of his visit—and still now, hours later. Was he going to think about her nonstop for the rest of his life?

Restless, he turned on the car radio and turned the dial. Nothing but scratchy country music and talk radio. Irritated, he flicked it off again and looked back at the school, then at the dashboard clock.

Any minute now, the kids would be here.

They could tell him every detail of their day, and he—

Well, he would tell them *some* details of his.

He'd leave out the part where he had driven past Dr. Klimek's old clinic after he'd left Sarah's. He'd slowed as he drove past, almost expecting to see Olivia's car in the parking lot. But of course it wasn't there. The place looked deserted. There was a FOR SALE sign out front.

Hearing voices through the closed car window, he looked up to see that the front doors of the school had finally opened and children were trickling out, calling to each other and carrying papers that fluttered in the snowy wind.

Max wondered if Sam and Lindsey would bring home drawings that he could hang on the fridge with magnets. He wondered if they'd have homework to do; whether they'd liked their teacher, Mrs. Starkey, whether they'd made friends.

Where *were* they?

He watched anxiously as other children burst out into the winter afternoon, running toward buses and parked cars and waiting mothers with bundled toddlers in their arms.

Then he spotted Lindsey's blond braids and Sam's red hat. They were walking together, with another child, the three of them laughing together.

So, they had made a friend already, Max thought, smiling.

A sense of well-being seeped in. His kids went to school and had friends. They were normal kids. Everything was going to be all right.

He watched them approach.

Lindsey looked up and spotted the Explorer. She broke into a run. Max opened the car door, mildly surprised that she was as eager to see him as he was to see her and Sam.

He stepped out into the gently falling snow, waving. "Hey, Lindsey! Sam! Hi, guys!"

"Daddy, you won't believe it!" Lindsey shouted, racing toward him. "You won't believe who was in our class!"

In that instant, Max recognized the little boy who, with Sam, had also broken into a run toward the Explorer.

His jaw dropped.

T.J.

Their new friend was T.J.

Olivia was still here in Newberry Cove.

It wasn't too late.

Max was flooded with emotion as he stood motionless, waiting for the children to reach him, knowing he couldn't betray his inner turmoil. Not here, not now.

"Hey, Sam," he said, crouching and catching his son, who had raced past Lindsey to arrive first.

"Hey, Lin'," he caught her, too, in his arms, squeezing them both in a brief hug.

Then he looked up at T.J., who had come to a halt a few feet away and was looking up at Max shyly.

"Hi, Max," the little boy said.

"T.J. . . ." He reached out and pulled the child into his embrace.

"Do you believe it, Daddy?" Lindsey was saying breathlessly. "He's in our class! Sam and me walked in and saw him sitting there and we were so surprised!"

"How come you told us he moved away?" Sam asked accusingly.

"Because I thought he had. I thought you and your mom had moved," Max told T.J., finally letting go of all three of them and standing again.

"Why'd you think that?" T.J. asked.

"I don't know. It was a mistake." *One of many,* he added to himself. And it was time to start undoing the damage he'd done. Time to make things right.

His heart was pounding. "I'm glad you didn't leave."

"I asked Mom if we could come visit you and she said no," T.J. offered. "I don't know why."

I do. But don't worry, buddy. I'm going to straighten things out. Just as soon as—

"T.J.!"

Her voice slammed into Max, knocking the wind out of him.

He turned and saw her there, on the sidewalk, only a few feet away.

"Olivia," he breathed, staring at her.

She had changed. Drastically.

Her hair—it was blond now, a tumble of pale, silken strands falling from beneath a red beret. The Olivia he had known would never have worn a jaunty red beret or those fuzzy red mittens. And her eyes—

That was the most striking change, he thought, mesmerized. They were blue. The clearest, truest blue he had ever seen. She must have worn colored lenses all this time. There was no sign of furtive fear in those eyes now. Only an expression he couldn't read.

"Hi, Max." She took a few steps toward him.

"I thought you moved away."

"No," she said hesitantly, and glanced at T.J., then back at him. He had the impression that she wanted to say something more, but didn't dare.

"Listen, guys," Max said, turning to the three children. "Why don't you go over there and build a snowman or something?" He motioned at the playground several yards away, where several kids were engaged in a good-natured snowball fight.

"Why is it always a snowman?" Lindsey asked. Sam had already taken off eagerly in the direction of the playground. "Why isn't it ever a snow-woman?"

"Snow-woman, then," Max said absently. "Just go."

"Can I go, too, Mom?" T.J. turned to Olivia, who hedged.

"I just want to talk to you," Max said to her in a low voice. "Just for a few minutes. Okay? Please?"

"Go ahead, T.J.," she told her son, and he and L̲i̲n̲d̲s̲e̲y̲ hurried after Sam.

When they were out of earshot, she looked back up at Max.

He didn't know what to say.

Apparently, neither did she. She chewed her lower lip. "So, you stayed," he finally said, lamely.

She nodded. "But only for a while. Until the school year is over. I didn't want to disrupt T.J.'s life."

His heart plummeted. "Where are you going?"

"I'm not sure, exactly. Probably south."

He nodded.

"I have to sell the clinic first. And Dr. Klimek's house. He left everything to me."

Startled, he looked up at her. "He did?"

"There was no one else. He had no family. So—he left it all to me and T.J."

"And you're selling everything?"

"What else can I do?"

Stay, he wanted to say. *Stay here. Please.*

Be here. With me.

Be . . .

"My wife," he heard himself say hoarsely.

She stared.

"Please, Olivia . . ." He got down on his knee in the snow, took her red-mittened hand in his leather-gloved one. "Please be my wife."

She opened her mouth. Closed it. Opened it.

"Max," finally came out. Then nothing else.

"I love you, Olivia. My God. I've loved you all along. I just never knew. I'm such a fool, such a—"

"No, Max."

Shattered, he slowly said, "No? You won't marry me?"

"No, I meant . . . you aren't a fool. I'm the fool. I should have come back to you the moment I realized how I felt—"

"You wanted to come back?"

She nodded, tears streaming down her cheeks. "I love you."

"You do?" he asked in disbelief, not daring to move, or breathe.

"I do. I love you. But I didn't think you—"

"I do, Olivia. I love you. I love you." He was giddy. He couldn't stop saying it. "I love you."

"Okay," she said, grinning. "I believe you."

"And you'll marry me?"

She answered with one word he couldn't possibly misunderstand. "Yes."

He stood and pulled her into his arms, holding her close.

Then he kissed her.

Her red beret fell off into the snow and neither of them cared.

They laughed.

He kissed her again, hungrily, running his fingers through her blond strands in wonder. She looked drastically different, yet he had the oddest sense of recognition. It was as though he had always known that this was who she was—this lighthearted blonde whose eyes were no longer haunted by the past, but instead held the promise of a future. *Their* future.

"We don't have to live out in the middle of nowhere," Max told her, in a rush to make plans.

"No, I want to. I want to live in your house. It's home," she told him. "And now I know that I've been homesick for months. I want to live there, and I want to be a mom to Sam and Lindsey. I want to be Mrs. Max Rothwell."

"Olivia Rothwell," he said, grinning down at her.

"No," she said, her eyes twinkling. "Katie. Katie Rothwell. Okay?"

He laughed and bent to kiss her again. "You bet. Katie. Kiss me, Katie."

Before his lips could meet hers, a snowball hit him squarely in the back.

"Sorry, Max," called T.J. guiltily.

He turned around. "That's 'Dad' to you, buddy. From now on. Okay?"

T.J.'s eyes widened. So did Sam's and Lindsey's.

"Come on," Max said to the future Katie Rothwell, tugging her hand and pulling her toward the playground. "Let's go build a snowman."

"Don't you mean a snow-*woman*?" she asked, her eyes twinkling.

"I'll tell you what . . . we'll build a snowman *and* a snow woman . . . a whole snow *family*." Then he added meaningfully, "And someday soon, we'll make some little snow babies, too. What do you think about that?"

"I think it's the best idea I've heard in a long time," she said, and she was laughing merrily as he kissed her again.

<u>BOOK YOUR PLACE ON OUR WEBSITE</u>
<u>AND MAKE THE</u>
<u>READING CONNECTION!</u>

We've created a customized website just for our very special readers, where you can get the inside scoop on everything that's going on with Zebra, Pinnacle and Kensington books.

When you come online, you'll have the exciting opportunity to:

- View covers of upcoming books
- Read sample chapters
- Learn about our future publishing schedule (listed by publication month *and author*)
- Find out when your favorite authors will be visiting a city near you
- Search for and order backlist books from our online catalog
- Check out author bios and background information
- Send e-mail to your favorite authors
- Meet the Kensington staff online
- Join us in weekly chats with authors, readers and other guests
- Get writing guidelines
- AND MUCH MORE!

Visit our website at
http://www.zebrabooks.com

Coming October 1999 From Bouquet Romances

#17 Somewhere In The Night by Marcia Evanick

__(0-8217-6373-3, $3.99) When Detective Chad Barnett finds Bridget McKenzie trembling at his door, the devastating memories of the case they worked on together five years ago come rushing back. While he can't deny the beautiful clairvoyant's plea for help, he knows he must resist the tender feelings she stirs in his heart.

#18 Unguarded Hearts by Lynda Sue Cooper

__(0-8217-6374-1, $3.99) Pro-basketball coach Mitch Halloran would have sent the gorgeous blonde bodyguard packing, but death threats were no joke—and Nina Wild didn't take "no" for an answer. But when Nina becomes the target of his stalker, he realizes she's the one woman in the world he isn't willing to lose.

#19 And Then Came You by Connie Keenan

__(0-8217-6375-X, $3.99) When attorney Cole Jaeger returns to Montana to sell the ranch he inherited from his uncle, he discovers one big problem—feisty beauty Sarah Keller, who not only lives at the ranch, but has the crazy notion that he's a rugged cowboy with a love of country life and a heart of gold.

#20 Perfect Fit by Lynda Simmons

__(0-8217-6376-8, $3.99) Wedding gown designer Rachel Banks creates dresses brides can only dream of, even if her own dreams have nothing to do with matrimony. But when blue-eyed charmer Mark Robison shows up at his sister's final fitting, sparks fly between the two.

Call toll free **1-888-345-BOOK** to order by phone or use this coupon to order by mail.

Name _____

Address _____

City _____ State _____ Zip _____

Please send me the books I have checked above.

I am enclosing $_____

Plus postage and handling* $_____

Sales tax (where applicable) $_____

Total amount enclosed $_____

*Add $2.50 for the first book and $.50 for each additional book.

Send check or Money order (no cash or CODs) to:

Kensington Publishing Corp., 850 Third Avenue, New York, NY 10022

Prices and Numbers subject to change without notice. Valid only in the U.S.

All books will be available 10/1/99. All orders subject to availability.

Check out our web site at **www.kensingtonbooks.com**

Celebrate Romance With Two of Today's Hottest Authors

Meagan McKinney

__The Fortune Hunter	$6.50US/$8.00CAN	0-8217-6037-8
__Gentle from the Night	$5.99US/$7.50CAN	0-8217-5803-9
__A Man to Slay Dragons	$5.99US/$6.99CAN	0-8217-5345-2
__My Wicked Enchantress	$5.99US/$7.50CAN	0-8217-5661-3
__No Choice but Surrender	$5.99US/$7.50CAN	0-8217-5859-4

Meryl Sawyer

__Half Moon Bay	$6.50US/$8.00CAN	0-8217-6144-7
__The Hideaway	$5.99US/$7.50CAN	0-8217-5780-6
__Tempting Fate	$6.50US/$8.00CAN	0-8217-5858-6
__Unforgettable	$6.50US/$8.00CAN	0-8217-5564-1

Call toll free **1-888-345-BOOK** to order by phone or use this coupon to order by mail.

Name _____
Address _____
City _____ State _____ Zip _____
Please send me the books I have checked above.
I am enclosing $_____
Plus postage and handling* $_____
Sales tax (in New York and Tennessee) $_____
Total amount enclosed $_____
*Add $2.50 for the first book and $.50 for each additional book.
Send check or money order (no cash or CODs) to:
Kensington Publishing Corp., 850 Third Avenue, New York, NY 10022
Prices and Numbers subject to change without notice.
All orders subject to availability.
Check out our website at **www.kensingtonbooks.com**

More Women's Fiction
From Kensington